NURK

URSULA VERNON

NURK

The Strange, Surprising Adventures of a (Somewhat) Brave Shrew

HARCOURT, INC.

Orlando   Austin   New York   San Diego   London

Requests for permission to make copies
of any part of the work should be submitted online
at www.harcourt.com/contact or mailed to the
following address: Permissions Department,
Houghton Mifflin Harcourt Publishing Company,
6277 Sea Harbor Drive, Orlando, Florida 32887-6777.

www.HarcourtBooks.com

Library of Congress Cataloging-in-Publication Data
Vernon, Ursula.
Nurk/Ursula Vernon.
p. cm.
Summary: Nurk, a sort-of brave shrew, packs up
a few pairs of clean socks and sails off on an accidental
adventure, guided by wisdom found in the journal
of his famously brave and fierce grandmother,
Lady Surka the warrior shrew.
[1. Adventure and adventurers—Fiction.
2. Shrews—Fiction. 3. Dragonflies—Fiction.
4. Courage—Fiction. 5. Diaries—Fiction.
6. Letters—Fiction.] I. Title.
PZ7.V5985Nur 2008
[Fic]—dc22   2007030788
ISBN 978-0-15-206375-7

Text set in Meridien
Designed by Linda Lockowitz

First edition
A C E G H F D B

Printed in the United States of America

For Thomas Maximilien McRudd

NURK

CHAPTER ONE

❻

"MoSt AdVEntUrES BeGin At hOME.
YoU dON't ReallY wAnT ThEm to,
bUt ThEy do AnyWaY."

—FROM THE JOURNAL OF SURKA AURELIA MAXINE SHREW

O N THE BANK OF A STREAM, on the edge of a forest, there lived a shrew named Nurkus Aurelius
Alonzo Electron Maximilian Shrew, which is
a hard thing for anyone to have to live with. Everyone
called him Nurk.

He was small and gray, and had small gray ears and a
small gray tail and enormous white whiskers that spread
out in a fan around his nose. He lived in a snug little house
under the roots of a whistling willow tree, and every evening he would sit on his front step and watch the stream
go rolling and roiling and rollicking by.

More than anything, Nurk wanted to be like his
grandmother Surka the warrior shrew. Surka had been
a fighter, a dishwasher, and a pirate queen, and he was

very proud to be related to her. Her portrait hung in his front hallway, and it was the first thing anyone saw when they entered his house. (Since the portrait showed her brandishing a severed head, this was a bit of a shock for first-time visitors, but Nurk's love for the portrait was un-dimmed.)

The problem was that he wasn't sure that he really wanted to have an adventure of his own. Most of the stories of adventure seemed to start somewhere very far away and skipped over the details of how you got there or what you were supposed to pack. They sounded messy and occasionally terrifying. Nurk was worried that he wouldn't go about having adventures the right way and would miss them entirely, or have a bad one where he spent most of his time wet and cold and hungry and with-out clean socks. Also he had to admit that he couldn't think of any situation where he would want to brandish anyone's severed head.

He wished that his grandmother was around to ask, but she had vanished long ago into the wild wibbling wastes, and no one had seen her since. He would have liked to talk to her, about adventures or anything else, and hear what she had to say. She had been very brave and very fierce, and Nurk suspected that he was neither, but it would have been nice just to see her again.

So for quite a while, Nurk was content to walk along the bank of the stream, kicking at pebbles and daydream-ing about the adventures he might someday have.

———

EVERYTHING CHANGED the day the letter arrived.

The letter was small and soggy and written in a nearly illegible hand, and it was being carried by the smallest, angriest hummingbird that Nurk had ever seen.

"Shrew," said the hummingbird, perching on a willow switch, which bobbed and swayed under the bird's weight. "Shrew. Willow tree. *Hmmph*." He fixed one small black eye on Nurk and then on the willow tree, then flicked his tail feathers as if to say that he'd seen better.

"Hello," said Nurk, who felt that it was important to be polite to government employees.

"*Hmmph*." The hummingbird dipped his long bill into the small sack of mail at his waist and pulled out a letter. "*Hmmph*. You Urk?"

"Errr . . . I'm Nurk . . ."

"Got a letter for an"—the hummingbird squinted at the address—"Urk. Shrew. Care of the Whistling Willow, Upstream." He frowned down at the little shrew. Since hummingbirds are mostly beak, the frown appeared to take up most of his body. "That you?"

"It might be." Nurk twisted his tail in his paws. "I'm a shrew, and this is the whistling willow, and my name is Nurk, so if they misspelled it—"

"*Hmmph*." The hummingbird eyed him with deep suspicion. "'Might be'? 'Might' isn't good enough. Letters have to go to the right person. Ad-dress-ee *only*. How do I know you're Urk?"

"Well . . . I'm *Nurk,* and I'm a shrew, and this is the whistling willow—"

"So you *say.*" The hummingbird waved the letter at him. "How do I know you're a shrew? You got any identification?"

Nurk glanced down at himself, baffled. No one had ever questioned whether he was a shrew before. It was generally considered self-evident. "Errr . . . what else could I be?"

The hummingbird drummed tiny claws on the willow twig. "Well . . . you might be a mouse pretending to be a shrew. Or a very cunning earthworm. Very important letter here. People might be trying to steal it."

"But I didn't even know I had a letter coming!" said Nurk, wondering exactly how cunning an earthworm would have to be to successfully impersonate a shrew.

"Aha!"

"'Aha' what?" Nurk was beginning to wonder if the letter was worth it. He rarely got mail, except for a birthday card from his great-aunt, and his birthday was months off. Still, he'd hate to miss a letter, and who else could it be for?

"Aha . . . er . . . *hmmph.*" The hummingbird apparently wasn't sure himself. "You're awfully *small* for a shrew."

Nurk thought this was a bit insulting, coming from a bird smaller than he was, but decided to let it pass.

"Are your parents home?"

"My parents are dead," said Nurk.

The hummingbird coughed, and the bit of skin at the edges of his beak flushed. "Didn't-know-sorry-for-your-loss," he muttered rapidly.

"It's okay," said Nurk. It had been several seasons since his parents were eaten by an owl, and he was beyond having to blink back tears when he thought about them. "But can I please have my letter?"

"*Hmmph.*" The hummingbird glared at him some more. "Do you swear you're Urk?"

"Actually I'm N— Yes, I swear." Nurk had no desire to go around the conversation another time.

"Okay." The hummingbird held out the letter. Nurk reached up for it, standing on the tips of his pink toes, but the hummingbird held it up out of reach.

"Now you do realize," said the bird gruffly, "that if you aren't Urk and you open a letter intended for someone else, you've committed theft and mail fraud and misrepresentation and swindling a public employee and using a false name and maybe even treason?"

"Goodness," said Nurk, who hadn't realized that at all.

"Right, then." The hummingbird dropped the letter into Nurk's paws and buzzed into the air. He hung suspended above the shrew's head, wings whirring. "Enjoy your letter, Mister Urk."

"It's Nurk—," the shrew began, but the hummingbird

was already flitting away, the afternoon light flickering on his jewel-toned feathers.

Nurk sighed and turned his attention back to the letter. The name on the envelope was badly smudged, as if it had gotten soaked in the rain. The only part that was clearly legible did indeed say "urk."

"Well, really," he said to himself, sitting down on his front step, "who else could it be for?" He pried the flap up with a claw and pulled out the message inside.

Water had seeped into the envelope and soaked the first few lines into a blur of ink. Two lines down, he began to make out words, occasionally interspersed with dark wet blobs.

> . . . don't know if you . . . still reach you here, but I'm hoping. . . . Please come at once! Father always said . . . need help, we could ask you. We need help now, as you can clearly . . . don't know why Father hasn't sent for you already . . . very sad. You have to help us save him! I only hope it's not too late.
>
> Please help us. If you can't, nobody can.

Nurk blinked.

This was clearly not a birthday card.

He read it twice through, but the words didn't change.

"Why would someone send me a letter asking for help?" he said, mostly to himself. He didn't know many people who didn't live nearby—his great-aunt and a few distant relatives, but that was all. Surely none of his neighbors, like the salamanders, would bother sending a letter—they'd just come and ask him for help.

And he couldn't imagine a situation where anyone would say that if he couldn't help them, nobody could.

He turned the letter over, looking for the return address, but it was badly smeared. It had to be someone downstream—they'd sent the letter to "Upstream," after all—but who could it have been?

And then his eye fell on the address, and he let out a tiny squeak.

What he'd taken for another blob of ink after the *k* in "urk" was suddenly obvious as an *a*. The letter was sent to "urka," and that almost certainly meant that it was sent to Surka, his grandmother, and that meant—

"I've opened someone else's mail," said Nurk in horror.

CHAPTER TWO

⑥

"YOU CAN'T FIGHT THE WEATHER.
WELL, YOU CAN—I'VE DONE it—bUT bEiNG sTrUCk
by liGHtNiNG iS oNLy FUn THE firSt
TWo oR ThReE tiMeS."

H E LEAPED TO HIS FEET, looking for the humming-bird—perhaps if he was still in sight, Nurk could return the letter and explain the misunderstanding—but the little bird was long gone. Not even a brightly colored speck dotted the sky.

"Mail fraud," moaned Nurk to himself, wringing his tail in his paws. "Theft and misrepresentation. Maybe even treason. Oh no. What am I going to *do*?"

He set the letter down on the step and edged away from it, as if it might bite. He needed advice, but he didn't know who to ask.

As if the thought had summoned him, there was a wet slapping sound, and the great spotted salamander that lived next door came eel-ling and oiling its way up the stream bank.

"Oh . . . ," said Nurk, fighting a sudden desire to hide the awful letter. "Oh, hello."

The salamander nodded to him. It had a name—at least, Nurk thought it was a name—in the bubbling salamander speech, but it sounded like "glub-glub-glub," and since all salamander words were some variation on "glub," Nurk had long since given up trying to pronounce his friend's name.

It didn't speak now but gazed distractedly up at the sky.

Still, the salamander had been living in the stream as long as Nurk could remember, and perhaps it had some advice about mail.

"Listen," said the little shrew, "I have this problem—a case of mistaken identity, really . . ."

The salamander listened gravely to Nurk's story, patting at the mud with its broad, soft fingers.

"So what do I dooooo?"

The salamander considered this at great length.

"Should deliver the letter," said the amphibian finally, ducking its head. "Send it on to the right person."

"But I don't know where she is!" said Nurk. "I don't even know if she's alive! Nobody's seen Grandma Surka in ages!"

"Oh." The salamander considered further, looking up at the sky again. "Should take the letter back, then."

"But I don't know who sent it!"

"Still." The salamander waved a hand distractedly

at him, staring up at the sky. Its throat was orange and pulsed when the salamander was nervous. It was pulsing now.

"Errr . . . is something wrong?" asked Nurk, after a moment. The salamander definitely seemed to have other things than mail fraud on its mind. Nurk could not imagine what on Earth would be more important than mail fraud, theft, and attempted treason, but then again, he wasn't a salamander.

The salamander dropped its head and looked at him. "There's a storm coming," it said. "The mud is unhappy."

Nurk wasn't sure how mud could be unhappy—or happy or anything else, since it was *mud*, after all—but the salamander seemed quite upset. The shrew peered up at the sky, but it was clear except for a few high clouds. "It doesn't look too much like a storm," he said.

"It's coming," said the salamander. "The water is fizzy and fretful against my skin, and the mud is unhappy between my toes. It will be the sort of storm that comes once in a century." It blinked its huge gold eyes solemnly and shivered.

The problem with talking to salamanders, Nurk had always found, was that while they were usually friendly, they lived in water as much as on land, and sometimes it was hard to understand what they were trying to say. It wasn't that they *tried* to be confusing, but salamanders think very differently than shrews, and sometimes what they mean by a word isn't what a shrew would mean.

Nurk could see that the salamander was making an effort to speak plainly, though, and the bit about the storm seemed clear enough. "Thank you," he said.

"Get down deep in the mud," said the salamander. "Get deep, deep down, where the storm won't go. I'm going down to the bottom of the stream. I'd go, too, if I were you."

"I'm not sure I can hold my breath that long," said Nurk doubtfully.

"Oh." The salamander sat back and thought about this for a long moment. "I'd still try," it said finally, and with a slap of its tail went wiggling and worming down the bank and *plop!* into the stream.

Nurk put his chin in his paw and considered.

It still didn't look much like a storm. The high clouds had been joined by a few more of their kind, and there was a bit of a breeze, but other than that, it was a perfectly pleasant evening, or would have been if he wasn't suddenly guilty of mail fraud.

Still, the salamander had gone out of its way to warn him. It couldn't hurt to be prepared.

Nurk went inside to close the windows and make sure he had plenty of candles.

A FEW HOURS LATER, he was glad that he had paid attention to the salamander's warning.

The storm had come raging in like a dragon made of clouds, breathing lightning and bellowing thunder. Rain lashed the ground and whipped the stream into a high froth. Nurk's whistling willow tree bent under the onslaught, until the creak of the wood sounded like a moan of pain.

Nurk thought about leaving the tree—if it was uprooted by the storm, it would be very unhealthy for anyone inside—but the tree had been in his family for generations. Since the unfortunate incident with the owl and his parents, Nurk had lived alone in the tree. An elderly great-aunt who lived on the other side of the island came by occasionally to check on him and make disapproving noises.

Still, for all that time, Nurk had made it a point of pride to keep up the willow. He cleaned the gutters and washed the windows, patched holes in the bark and weeded the front walk. The willow was part of the family. He couldn't just abandon it.

Staring out the front window as the tree shuddered and creaked, Nurk could see a lot of repairs in his future.

"Assuming I even have a future and the post office doesn't come and take me away for stealing Grandma Surka's letter."

He sighed.

The irony was that Grandma Surka probably wouldn't have cared that he had opened her mail. He hadn't seen her since he was very, very small, but his memory was of a wild, laughing, larger-than-life figure who was utterly disdainful of such minor details and who drank acorn milk right out of the carton. (This had been very impressive to Nurk as a child, and it had taken months for his mother to break him of the habit.)

"Should take the letter back, then," the salamander had said.

"The salamander doesn't know how far it is," Nurk muttered to himself. "It's downstream. How would I get there? I don't even know who sent it . . ."

Even if he did somehow find the person who'd written the letter, what if they were angry? It was obviously important—they'd been begging Surka for help. They'd be awfully disappointed to get Nurk instead.

Worse yet: "What if they expect *me* to help them?"

It would be an adventure, all right, but this sounded serious. He was only a little shrew.

Even Surka had to start somewhere, said a traitorous little voice in his head. He ignored it.

"I've got trouble enough already . . . mail fraud, theft, possibly treason . . ."

And that was another problem—what if he tried to return the letter, and instead of being grateful, they had him arrested for opening it in the first place? How badly did they punish you for opening someone else's mail by accident? Did they give you a stern look, or did they feed you to owls? Nurk didn't know.

Maybe it would be better just to shove the letter under a stack of papers and pretend it never existed.

But it had sounded *really* important. . . . The shrew twisted his tail in his paws in an agony of guilt.

Creeeeeaaaaaaaaaaaakk . . . !

Something hit the door with a bang and Nurk jumped. Thunder rattled the windows. When he peered out, during the brief flashes he could see broken branches flying through the air. He edged away from the window.

"Maybe the salamander was right," he said to himself.

There was only one place where he could get deep, deep down in the tree, and that was in the root cellar. Taking a candle and a bag of pistachios, and making sure all the other lamps were out, Nurk went to the stairs and pulled open the door to the root cellar. The creak of the hinges was lost in the creaking of the willow tree.

Just as the tree had been the home of shrews for generations, the cellar had been the home of their junk. Old trunks and boxes were piled along the walls, rising in cardboard columns over Nurk's head. Bins were buried under drifts of broken toys, unmatched dishes, headless hammers, orphaned jigsaw puzzle pieces, and keys to unknown locks. There was a whole box full of broken whisker brushes (shrews have very long whiskers and groom them as carefully as other people brush their teeth) and another box that looked like the final resting place for six generations of kitchen junk drawers.

It was gloomy in the cellar, but it was also much quieter and the floor didn't sway. The creak of the willow was still audible but not so loud. Nurk set the candle on a trunk, shelled a few pistachios, and began rummaging in the trunks for some way to amuse himself until the storm blew over and to stop himself from thinking about that awful letter.

The first box contained some very bad paintings of fruit, and the second box was full of baby clothes. The third box was full of books, which Nurk was initially excited by, but they turned out to be old scrapbooks from a side of the family he'd never met. He flipped through one, saw no one he recognized, and sighed.

He was trying to get the scrapbooks back in—putting a thing back in the box is never as easy as getting it out in the first place—when another book tumbled out of the box and landed on his foot.

Nurk picked it up. It was a small leather-bound book with a lock. There was no writing on the covers. The lock had long since broken (which was a good thing, because even with all the keys lying around, he didn't know how long it might have taken to find the correct one), and when he flipped it open, he saw that it was handwritten in a bold but sloppy hand.

On the inside cover, the book said: "PrOpeERty oF sUrKA aUReliA maXinE sHrew." Underneath it was a drawing of a severed head.

It was his grandmother's journal.

CHAPTER THREE

⑥

"pEnMAnShiP Is FoR ThE weAK."

THE STORM CONTINUED to rage overhead, but Nurk was oblivious to it. The candle burned down, and he lit another one. The tree creaked, and Nurk paid no attention. A small pile of pistachio shells grew at his feet, but he barely tasted the nuts.

Once he'd gotten over the initial rush of guilt—was it a sign? Had the journal fallen on him as some kind of punishment from Surka's ghost for stealing her mail? No, surely not, Grandma Surka wouldn't care, and if she did, her supernatural vengeance would have been a lot more dramatic than a falling book—he'd been much too curious not to read it.

The journal was fascinating.

Well, it was probably fascinating.

The pictures were certainly interesting. Surka had sketched more than a few of the creatures that she had encountered in her travels, and they were all different sorts—delicate little beings with big eyes and feathery ankles, gigantic warty beasts like frogs with horns, slithery slimy things with mouths full of jagged teeth. Nurk longed to meet some of them and devoutly hoped he would never meet others.

The writing, though . . .

His grandmother had, by all accounts, been a top-notch warrior, but this skill apparently didn't translate into penmanship. The direction of the letters *S* and *R* appeared to have been determined by flipping a coin. She capitalized things at random and had a pirate's distrust of punctuation.

There was a definite take-no-prisoners attitude to her spelling, though. Surka spelled words as if they had personally offended her.

For Nurk, reading the journal was not so much like reading a book as it was like trying to decipher a complicated code. Some of the words were completely illegible, so he had to figure them out from the context, and since Surka had been writing a great many seasons before, some of the words were old and archaic, and he had to decipher their meanings.

Still, after an hour or two, while the willow tree groaned and wax slipped slowly down the candle to puddle on the wood, Nurk had managed to translate the first page, and when he finally read it all the way through, it struck him like a lightning bolt.

THIS is THE jOURNaL OF SUrKa AUrelia MAXine ShREw, it read. i aM kEepiNG iT to REcorD mY trAVels, as I hAVe detErmiNeD to seT oUt on mY owN AnD sEEk AdVentURe. My paRenTS hAve toLd mE To waiT uNtil I Am oLDer, buT I Have beEn wAitinG lonG enoUgh. IT seEms to me ThAt if I kEEp wAitinG uNtiL I aM oLDeR, oNe daY i'LL dIscoveR thAt I aM oId, aNd I wiLl <u>sTiLL</u> not hAve HaD aN AdVenTuRe!

I hAve Had mANy dReamS, bUt I have dECideD to stoP. MY sister aLso dReAmeD of adVEnTuRe, aNd eVeNTuaLLy sHe hAd so maNy dReAms ThAt sHe Didn'T waNt to haVe a ReaL aDVentuRe, FoR feAr oF spoIliNG ThEm. ThiS wiLl <u>noT</u> hAppeN to mE!

I dO noT kNow iF I wiLl suRViVe, aS aDVentuReS aRe peRiLoUs ThinGs, aNd if I aM deVouREd By hUngRY cRocoDiLes or maDdeNed eGgpLaNtS, theY wiLl pRoBably not ALLow mE tiME to reCord a LaSt enTRy. In ThE cASe thAt ThiS JouRnaL iS loCateD in thE deN of a maDdeNEd egGPlanT oR thE STomacH oF a cRocoDile, pLeAsE RetUrn to my FaMily at thE WhiSTlinG WiLLow. i hAVE

(This section was completely illegible and looked as if Surka had been trying to kill a flea with the tip of the pen.)

mE luCk.

AdVeNturE aWAitS!

———

NURK SAT BACK and let his breath out slowly.

Despite the words having been written fifty seasons or more ago, it felt as if his grandmother was speaking directly to him. It was as if she had reached clear across time to grab him by the scruff of the neck and yell, "Pay attention!"

He had been sitting and waiting for adventure, he thought. Dreaming about it, like Surka's sister. (He wasn't sure which of his great-aunts that sister had been—Minerva, maybe, who had had fifteen children and never went more than a mile from her tree.)

And now an adventure had fallen into his lap. "Should take the letter back, then," the salamander had said. He *should* take the letter back. *Surka* would have taken the letter back.

It would be a long way, and he wasn't entirely sure where he was going or how to get there. He'd never been downstream in his life. But still—

IT seEMs to me ThAt if I kEeP wAitinG uNtiL I aM oLDeR, oNe daY i'LL diScoveR thAt I aM olD, aNd I wilL STiLL not hAVe HaD aN AdVenTuRe!

The words were like icy water thrown on his fur. Nurk was shocked and chilled and yet energized. He leaped to his feet, scattering pistachio shells.

He would have an adventure. He would return the letter. He would avoid getting arrested for mail fraud and make his grandmother proud in the bargain. And if they yelled at him—well, he'd deal with that. He would go.

He would go *now*.

A particularly loud crack of thunder rocked the floor, and the tree moaned like a dying animal.

Well, perhaps not right this minute.

"Soon, though," said Nurk aloud, to the room full of boxes and broken toys. "I'll go soon."

THE STORM BLEW itself out by morning, and Nurk got up early, his neck cramped from sleeping in the cellar. He had tried to decipher a bit more of the journal but found it rough going, and anyway, he'd been too excited and nervous to sit still for long. He was determined to have an adventure and to have one soon.

Once he got out of the cellar, though, it seemed like his adventure might be a bit delayed. Although the whistling willow had come through the storm mostly intact, the roof of his kitchen had sprung a leak, and Nurk spent most of the morning mopping up an inch of rain from the tiles.

When he went outside at last, the stream bank seemed strangely cluttered. Branches and debris had been blown in from the storm and washed up on the shore. Instead of smooth sand and pebbles, there were piles of twigs and dead leaves everywhere.

Intrigued by this strange new landscape, Nurk went for a walk along the bank. Every few feet, he had to scramble over branches or walk around a tangle of water weeds.

Then, far ahead, he saw something strange washed up on the bank of the stream. At first it looked like a stone, and then it looked like a turtle, and for a little bit it even looked like a tuba—Nurk wasn't sure what a tuba would be doing on the banks of his stream, but stranger things have happened—and finally he got close enough to see what it really was.

It was a snail shell.

The outside of the shell was rust and orange, dripped and drabbed with dark brown spots. The inside was smooth and dry and empty.

Nurk peered deep inside. "Hello?" he called, and *hello hello hellll . . . oooh . . .* echoed inside the shell, but there was no one there.

"I wonder how the shell got here," said Nurk. "I suppose it must have been washed here by the storm . . ."

And then Nurk had an idea. It hit him all at once, and he stood very still and very quiet, as if the idea were a butterfly that had landed on his head. After a long, long moment, when he was sure that the idea wasn't going to escape, he let out a slow breath and examined the snail shell more closely.

If the shell could float, why not a shrew? The shell was a neat curving spiral more than big enough for a shrew to crawl inside. He could make a boat and sail down the stream, and—if he was lucky—find an adventure.

"*Hmm,*" Nurk said. "I wonder . . ."

CHAPTER FOUR

❦

"i LoVE BoAtS. bOaTS aRe GrEaT.
yoU cAn gEt aLl kiNdS oF pLacEs AnD mEeT aLl kinDs
oF iNTeREStInG pEoPLe, aNd YoU nEveR kNow iF tHEy'Re
GoiNg to tRy To eAt yoU oR woRShiP you aS The
goD oF sHreWs CoME dOwN fROm oN HigH."

OR THE NEXT WEEK, Nurk worked on the snail shell all day, every day, from early in the morning to far into the night.

He cut a mast and tied it to the shell. He made oars out of ginkgo leaves, and an anchor from a hollow acorn filled with pebbles. He even spent a very long day melting pine sap in a pot and smearing it on the shell to make it extra-watertight. This was his only cooking pot, and it took him a long time to get the pine sap out of it, so he had to live on cold cereal and cheese and crackers for several days until he had scrubbed it clean again, and even so, his morning oatmeal tasted a bit like pine for weeks afterward.

Nurk sawed and hammered and sanded and chopped

until he was exhausted and there were blisters on his paws. It was the hardest work he had ever done in his life, and the ointment he put on his blisters was awful stuff that smelled like an orange had been violently ill. It made his whiskers curl themselves into knots. But whenever he thought of giving up, he remembered his grandmother Surka and his wish to have an adventure.

Then he would get up and go back to work again.

The snail shell, he was sure, would be just the thing for having adventures in, even if he didn't have any severed heads to put in it.

The salamander came over most days to see how the snail shell was coming along and to occasionally offer advice. Some of it was cryptic salamander talk—"The boat must love the water, if the water is to love the boat"—but some of it was useful advice, and his amphibious friend helped him slide it onto rollers so that Nurk could crawl underneath and smear pine sap on the bottom.

At night, once it got so dark that Nurk was hammering his thumb more often than the nails, he would pull leaves over the snail shell to protect it from rain and then trudge home. By candlelight, he would read more of his grandmother's journal.

One passage early on said:

I hAve TakEn a BoaT to ThE iSLanDs. ThE BOat iS caPTAinEd BY a dRunKen HeDGehoG wHo siNgs TeRrible SonGs, bUt hE is ThE oNLy CaPtAin wHo WiLL ViSit ThE iSLanDs. THErE aRe rePorTs oF moNsTerS oN ThosE sHorES, wHiCh makE terRIblE rOArinG soUndS At NiGht anD eAt unWarY trAvelErs. I aM eXcitEd to MEet THeM.

Nurk found the line about the boat comforting, even if the bits about the monsters weren't. (The following pages were completely unreadable, but the pictures had a lot of teeth.) Obviously boats were an acceptable method of getting to an adventure, and he was bound to be a better captain than a drunken hedgehog.

When he was too tired to read anymore, he would go to bed and sleep so soundly his tail didn't even twitch.

By the time the ship was finally done, Nurk was beside himself with excitement. He could hardly sleep the night before. In the morning he got up very early and took a bottle of root beer out to the ship.

He was so eager to be off, he could hardly wait until the patient salamander came wriggling out of the muck, its great golden eyes half-lidded with sleep.

Nurk nodded to the salamander, feeling very important—the salamander dipped its head politely in reply—and broke the bottle over the prow. (It took two tries.) "I name this the Snailboat!" Nurk cried. The salamander applauded, slapping its tail loudly against the mud.

Nurk was very proud. The ship was small and snug and watertight, and just the sort of thing to have an adventure in, and it also didn't immediately fall apart under the root-beer bottle, which he considered a very good sign.

Nurk packed some sandwiches and a raincoat, his

knapsack, a towel, and an extra pair of socks. He wasn't sure what else he was supposed to take on an adventure, so he took a pillow and a blanket in case he had to sleep in the Snailboat, and his cooking pot, and a tin of oatmeal in case he needed breakfast, and a pair of scissors because he couldn't count the number of times he'd been out somewhere and really needed a pair of scissors. He packed it all up in the spiraling interior of the snail shell, and then looked at it for a while, and then went and got two more pairs of socks, just in case. He didn't know what kind of adventure he would have, but he knew that very few things are much fun when all you can think about is how wet and cold your feet are. He would almost rather have dealt with severed heads.

Last but not least, he took the letter, with its illegible return address, and set it carefully inside.

Once the Snailboat was packed, he went over the whistling-willow tree very carefully, making sure that the doors were locked and his bed was made and there were no dishes tucked in odd corners of the house that would grow mold. He wasn't sure how long he would be gone, so he wrote a note for his great-aunt in case she came by to check on him.

> Gone downstream to return a letter. Will return as soon as possible.
>
> Your Obedient Nephew,
> Nurkus Aurelius Shrew

He sat back and chewed on the end of his pencil. Should he say anything more? Aunt Wilhelmina had gone a little way upstream in her youth and considered herself a great traveler, but she also had a bad habit of treating Nurk like a small child. If he explained that he didn't know whom the letter belonged to or where he was going—no, best to keep it simple. The last thing his adventure needed was Aunt Wilhelmina turning up at an inopportune moment, brandishing her umbrella, and demanding to know what in the name of Saint Soricidae he thought he was doing.

He left the note on the kitchen table, looked around one more time, and then went out the front door and shut it behind him. "I'll be back," he promised the tree, patting the trunk with a paw. "Once I deliver this letter. I promise."

Finally, he opened his grandmother's diary, completely at random, and read the first line that was legible.

i aM gLAd +O Be GoiNg. TheY SAy THeRe aRe bLUe CHickeNs thERe!

"I doubt there'll be blue chickens downstream," said Nurk to himself, "but I suppose you never know." For all he knew, the letter had been written by a blue chicken. The line seemed like a good omen, anyway, since he was also glad to be going somewhere.

Then he climbed into the Snailboat.

The salamander, who had been loitering in the water while Nurk packed, grabbed the lead rope and towed the

Snailboat out into the middle of the stream. "The water is happy today," it informed Nurk.

"Good to know," said the shrew.

The amphibian paused, tail fanning in the current, and then lifted one wet hand, closed its great eyes, and murmured something in the glubbing language of salamanders. Nurk wasn't sure if it was a prayer, a blessing, or the amphibian equivalent of "Write if you find work," but he was touched all the same.

"Water's luck to you," the salamander said, opening its eyes and dropping the rope. It waved.

"Thank you for your help! Good-bye!" called Nurk, waving back.

Nurk put the Snailboat's oars in the water and began to row.

It was hard work. If you're not used to rowing, it's *very* hard work, and the worse you are at it, the harder it is. Nurk was a strong little shrew, but he had never rowed before, and he soon grew tired and pulled the oars in.

"I hope it's time to raise the sail," he said.

So he raised the sail. It was made of patchwork, since Nurk hadn't had any really big pieces of fabric lying around, and parts of it were still identifiable as old shirts, dishrags, and socks with holes in them. But it caught the wind as well as any sail made of canvas, and the Snailboat began to speed along at a good clip.

Soon the Snailboat reached the current and began to go faster and faster. The salamander, Nurk's house, and

even Nurk's tree soon vanished into the distance behind them.

Nurk had never traveled so fast in his life. (Given that the previous owner was a snail, the Snailboat probably hadn't ever traveled so fast, either.) Wind whipped past his ears and tickled his whiskers. As he peered around, clutching the edges of the snail shell for dear life, the Snailboat shot down the stream.

He was so busy looking around that he forgot to look ahead, and so he didn't see the rocks until much too late. The Snailboat wallowed in the water like an injured fish. Nurk squeaked in terror and fell back in the shell, but he could still see the rocks looming up on either side. They were twice as large as the Snailboat and pointed and jagged and terrible.

There was an awful wailing *skreeeeeek* as the snail shell scraped on stone.

"Noooo!" Nurk cried, clutching his tail. He was afraid for himself, but more than that, he couldn't bear the thought of the Snailboat, that he'd worked so hard on, getting a hole less than ten minutes into its maiden voyage.

Skeeeeeek—skreeeeee—THUMP!

"This was not a good idea," moaned Nurk from the bottom of the boat.

Splash!

It took Nurk a long minute to realize that he was okay, that the Snailboat had skimmed through the rocks, and that the stream was flowing into a much broader, quieter waterway. He sat up and scanned the horizon but saw no more rocks. Then, dreading what he might find, he went below and checked the inside of the shell.

Amazingly, it all looked dry and snug as ever, even when he pushed the blankets aside and went over every inch of the shell with his paws.

"We were pretty lucky," he said to the Snailboat, coming back out into the open. "Must have been the pine sap. But what's this stream? And how are we going to get back home?"

Looking back, though, Nurk realized that his tree had actually been on a large island between the stream and the river. "I never knew I lived on an island," he said. His Aunt Wilhelmina always said that travel broadened the mind—she considered herself to be *very* broad-minded— and Nurk had always thought that meant you needed to buy bigger hats (Aunt Wilhelmina, herself, wore enormous hats with plastic fruit on them). But maybe she had meant something like this instead. Perhaps when he came back, he could go up the river, instead of the stream, and then walk back across the island to home.

Assuming, that is, Nurk could figure out how to go up the river at all. The ginkgo-leaf oars looked very small and flimsy to set against the rolling current.

Still, at the moment, downriver seemed like a good direction to go, particularly since that direction seemed to involve the least rowing.

Besides, the return address on the letter said "Downstream," so downstream Nurk would go.

The river was wide and much slower than the stream Nurk lived on. The Snailboat slowed its headlong flight and began to move steadily but not too fast.

It was a very relaxing pace. The scenery unrolled on either side—green fields, edged with cattails and reeds, swaying and dipping in the wind. Little brown birds flitted among the reeds and occasionally stopped and cocked their heads and looked down at the little shrew in the Snailboat that went sailing by. They chirped questions at each other, but the Snailboat sailed on so that Nurk didn't hear the answers.

The fields were so relaxing to watch, and the motion of the Snailboat was a gentle rocking—and he was, after all, very tired from rowing—so it's not surprising that Nurk soon fell asleep in the bottom of the Snailboat, without even unpacking his pillow.

CHAPTER FIVE

6

"yoU FinD fRienDS in The MoST uNeXpEcTed pLAces.
EneMieS, too, FoR thAt MatTeR."

IT WAS MUCH, MUCH LATER, getting on toward evening, when the Snailboat ran aground with a *thump!* on a log submerged in the middle of the river. The thump woke Nurk up immediately, and he jumped to his feet, which is never a wise thing to do in a boat. The Snailboat rocked dangerously, and he barely missed hitting his head on a branch, so he sat down and grabbed his tail in his paws and twisted it.

"This isn't good," he said. "This isn't good at all."

He was caught up in the middle of the river. The log was a great tangle of branches, both under and over the water, so it was rather like running aground on a large waterlogged hedgehog. Everywhere he looked were spiky twigs and branches, including one that ran right over the opening in the Snailboat, so he had to keep ducking. He didn't know how he was going to get free, and it was nearly dark out, and to make matters worse, he had a crick in his neck from sleeping without his pillow.

Nurk put his paws on the edge of the shell and peered into the gloom. The rolling fields had been replaced by a dark and desperate forest. He could hear an owl calling somewhere in the distance, and that worried him, because owls are very large and very quiet and very, *very* hungry, and his family did not have a good history with them.

Surka's diary was sitting by his foot. He picked it up, for it was rapidly growing too dark to read.

He consulted it, the same way as before, by picking a passage at random. With his eyes closed, he flipped it open and poked a finger at the page.

When he opened his eyes, the line he was pointing to read:

I bELieVe TRoLLs to bE deSCeNdeD FroM BiLLY GoATs, wHiCh woULd exPlaiN ThE FeUd beTWeEn THeM. DeSPitE tHEiR siZE aNd FeARSoMe APPeaRanCe, tHE tRoLLs aRe VErY good-nAtUrEd. THeY hAve MaDE me THeIR cHieF!

This did not seem helpful.

"What am I going to do?" he wondered aloud, his small knuckles going white where he gripped the rim of the snail shell.

"You could let me on board," somebody answered from directly below the boat.

"*Yeeerrriip!*" squeaked Nurk, jumping backward. The Snailboat rocked.

"And stop doing that," said the voice. "You're splashing me."

The voice was scratchy and raspy and metallic, like sand poured into a copper kettle. Nurk had never heard a voice like it. It might have been a perfectly nice voice in broad daylight, but in the twilight, when Nurk was far from home, hung up on logs, and worried about owls, the voice was very scary.

"Stay back!" he cried. "I have—um—socks!"

There was a pause while the voice considered this threat.

"Dirty or clean?" it asked.

"Clean," Nurk was forced to admit.

"Then I'm afraid I'm not very scared of your socks," said the voice. "Dirty socks, maybe. Clean socks, however, are just not scary."

"You have a point," said Nurk.

"Do you suppose I could come aboard?" asked the voice. "I'm extremely cold and wet, and I've been clinging to this log for quite a long time."

Nurk thought about how he'd feel if he had been clinging to a log for a long time and decided he might not be nearly so calm as the voice was being. If it was a monster, it was a very polite one. "Okay," he said, "but slowly." He grabbed one of the oars, just in case it turned into a severed-head sort of situation.

Two delicate green hands closed on the rim of the Snailboat. Nurk examined them closely. They were smaller than Nurk's paws, and the nails were neatly trimmed and painted purple. That particular shade of

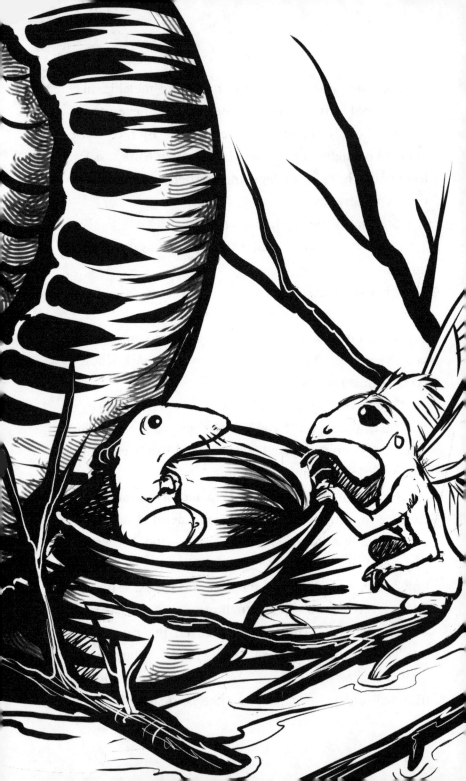

purple was admittedly rather monstrous, but Nurk figured he'd better give the owner the benefit of the doubt.

And then, rather alarmingly, *another* set of identical hands settled on the rail, one on either side of the first set.

"How many hands do you *have*?" asked Nurk worriedly.

"The usual number. Four," said the voice. "Why, how many do you have?"

"Two."

"Weird."

Then the hands pulled their owner up, and Nurk found himself face-to-face with a dragonfly.

The dragonfly was no bigger than he was, a little reptilian creature with four arms and two legs, enormous orange eyes, and a dusting of tiny metallic scales. She was mostly sea-foam green, but there were black markings down the backs of her arms, and her hair looked like it was probably bright red and yellow when it wasn't soaking wet and hanging in limp tangles.

Even Aunt Wilhelmina and her fruit hats—which she wore with enormous, brightly colored gowns in a cacophony of colors—could not compare with the vividness of the dragonfly.

Her wings were soaking wet and hung from her shoulders like soggy, crumpled paper. She frowned over her shoulder at them, then turned back to Nurk.

"You're a shrew!" she said.

"My name is Nurk," said Nurk. "I'm trying to have an adventure."

"I am the Princess of Dragonflies," she said, squeezing water out of her hair.

"Um." Nurk wasn't quite sure what you said after somebody announced they were a princess. ("Neat!" didn't seem to quite cover it.) "Hi." He cast around for something else to say and came up with "Nice nail polish."

"Thanks!" she said. "It's Gorgeous Grape."

Nurk privately thought that it looked more like Ghastly Grape or Grotesque Grape, maybe even Gag-Inducing Grape, but figured he should keep that to himself. He'd never met a dragonfly before; maybe they all liked weird nail polish. He found his towel and handed it to her.

"Thank you." She began drying her feet, which had two large toes each, also with purple nails. "People usually call me Scatterwings."

"It's nice to meet you."

"So how did you get stuck?" Scatterwings asked.

"I fell asleep in the Snailboat," he admitted. "I've never been sailing before."

"You're lucky all you did was get stuck," she said.

"I suppose. But I don't know how to get loose—the tangle just goes on and on, and even if I get unstuck from this bit here, I'm afraid I'll just get stuck on the next one."

"*Hmm,*" said Scatterwings. "There's not much point in getting unstuck tonight, even if we could—we couldn't see where we were going. But if I can sleep on top of your

Snailboat and spread my wings out on the shell so they dry, tomorrow I can fly to my father's palace and get help."

"That sounds great!" said Nurk.

So the two agreed to the plan and had a late dinner of cheese sandwiches, and then Nurk helped Scatterwings crawl up the round dome of the Snailboat. She stretched out her wings to either side—they were very large when she spread them, almost as big as the sail of the Snailboat—and set them to dry. Nurk gave her his pillow, since the shell of the Snailboat couldn't be very comfortable, and even though neither one was quite as cozy as they could have been, they both fell asleep almost at once.

NURK WOKE UP in a bad mood. Sleeping without a pillow can make anyone grumpy, and it was colder out on the water than he had expected. To make matters worse, Scatterwings snored, a piercing, groggling, echoing snore like someone yodeling down a drainpipe.

Nurk had never met a princess before, and most of what he knew about princesses involved fairy tales about delicate creatures who slept on feather beds and danced all night in silk slippers. He did not recall any of the fairy tales mentioning a snore that could have penetrated concrete. Obviously Scatterwings was just not that sort of princess.

"Travel broadens the mind," he muttered, pulling the blanket over his head. "How wonderful."

By the time Nurk finally gave up on sleep and got up,

it was barely dawn and the air was dim and damp and cold.

He wrapped his blanket around his shoulders and sat in the prow of the Snailboat, nibbling on a sandwich. This did not improve his mood. Cheese sandwiches are a good thing, like clean socks, but neither one is very good for breakfast, particularly when they're cold and starting to get stale. Unfortunately, there was no place to build a fire to cook oatmeal in the middle of the river, and starting a fire on the Snailboat did not seem like a particularly good idea.

He wondered how long it would take to find the owner of the letter. What if he went without breakfast for days? What if he had to eat cheese sandwiches for weeks?

Nurk sat and felt rather sorry for himself. In the background, Scatterwings continued to snore.

He consulted Surka's diary again, but the passage was a long complaint about the quality of the food in some place called the Outer Hebrides, and the drawings all featured a shrew, presumably Surka, making horrible faces.

As Nurk sat sulking, the sun came up, a little at a time, and cast pale gold and pink flecks on the silvery surface of the river. Mist was curling and curving over the water, moving in little skittering puffs with the breeze. It was really very pretty, but Nurk was in no mood to appreciate it.

And then—

"HNAAAAGH!"

The sound was so loud and booming and unexpected that Nurk fell over on his tail. The blanket got tangled up in his ears and whiskers, and it took a minute before he managed to poke his long nose out of the blankets and, very carefully, over the rim of the Snailboat.

"HNAAAGH!" came again (Nurk squeaked in surprise) and then "hnaagh, hnaagh, HNAAGH!" came back from all over the river, a whole chorus of deep, gurgling voices.

Nurk, still with the blanket mostly over his head, peered around the river. It took him three tries to see the source of the noises, because they were the color of the water and the mud and the stones. When he finally saw them, he felt silly for having been so startled.

"Frogs!" cried Nurk.

"Hnaaaagh!" bellowed the frogs.

". . . snoooorrrrrghgghraaghghe . . . ," snored Scatterwings from the roof.

As Nurk watched, the frogs gathered together a few yards downriver. The biggest frogs sat down in the water, and smaller frogs perched on the bank of the river, on the submerged branches, and occasionally on top of the other frogs. The tiniest frog was as bright green as a new leaf, and it perched high on a twig sticking out from the pile of submerged logs.

All together, in a great gurgling harmony, the frogs began to sing.

"Hnaagh!"

"Hnaagh!"

"Hnaaaagh-a-raaaagh!"

"Hnaagh!"

"Hnaaaaaaagh!"

"HNAAAGH!"

The littlest frog had a peeping voice like a tiny flute, and it sang, *"Hnagh-hnagh-hnagh!"* overhead.

Nurk was enchanted. He knew he'd never have seen anything like this on his island, and his bad mood dried up and blew away like a leaf in the wind. "Travel really does broaden the mind!" he said to himself, and wondered if someday he would be telling young shrews about his adventure on the river, while wearing a hat with plastic fruit on it.

The frogs ended their song with one great *"Hhhnaaaagggggggghhh!"* all together, like an amphibian pipe organ, and then, one by one, they hopped into the water—*splish splash sploosh!*—and swam away. Only the littlest frog remained, clinging to his twig with his eyes closed tightly, humming happily to himself.

Overhead, Scatterwings snored on.

CHAPTER SIX

❻

"THERe's NOTHiNG qUiTe As inSPiRiNg As A
wHoLe gRouP OF cReAtuRes coMiNg toGeTheR
to AcComPLiSH soME gReAT woRk.
I coULd siT aNd wATcH it aLL dAy."

By the time the dragonfly woke up, the sun was high in the sky and her wings were no more than damp. But the full daylight had revealed just how hung up the little Snailboat was. Branches crossed the sky like prison bars around them. Nurk didn't see how they could ever get loose.

"Not to worry!" said Scatterwings, who had woken up very cheerful. Nurk tried not to hold this against her. "My wings are almost dry, see?" She flexed one. It looked like beautifully patterned tissue paper. "I'll be ready to fly in just a few minutes. Then I'll go see my dad, the king, and he'll get this all sorted out."

"How did you end up in the river in the first place?" asked Nurk curiously.

"The wind blew me right into the water." Scatter-wings crossed both pairs of arms across her chest, looking defensive. "It's true."

The funny thing was if she hadn't said, "It's true," Nurk would have believed her. But when somebody feels obligated to say, "It's true," it makes you wonder why.

She was probably doing something she wasn't supposed to do, he thought, and she's embarrassed to admit it.

Whether this was true or not, the next few minutes passed in rather awkward silence. Scatterwings poked around the cabin. Nurk stood at the front of the boat and tried to figure out how the Snailboat could be pried loose.

It didn't look good. There were twigs jammed in on all sides, including a few behind them that had apparently drifted in during the night. The Snailboat looked as if it were encased in a basket woven by someone with more enthusiasm than skill.

"*Hmm,*" Nurk said, peering over the edge, "I wonder if—"

Whatever he might have been wondering was lost as Scatterwings yelped from inside the cabin.

Nurk whirled around. "Are you okay?"

"Okay? *Okay?*" The dragonfly princess advanced on him, flushing the color of old bronze. "This is my letter!" She waved the envelope furiously at him. "How did *you* get my letter? Oh, I knew I shouldn't have trusted that hummingbird!"

"This is *your* letter?" Nurk practically squealed with delight. "That's wonderful! I opened it by mistake, and I wanted to find whoever sent it to return it, and I didn't know where to find them, but if it's *your* letter—"

"No! You don't understand! This is horrible! This is the worst possible thing that could happen!" The dragonfly sat down in the bottom of the boat and wrapped her wings around her head.

Faced with a sudden wall of iridescent silence, Nurk said, "Errr."

This was awful. Nurk suspected that she might be crying. He had thought that someone might yell at him for opening the letter, but never in his worst nightmares had he thought someone might cry at him.

After a minute, when it became obvious that Scatterwings wasn't coming out, Nurk located something that looked like her shoulder and patted it. "Um. I'm sorry. I didn't mean to open your letter. It looked like it was addressed to me . . ."

"You're not Surka," she said, her voice muffled with wings and tears. "She's not coming to help us."

"Surka's my grandmother."

There was a long pause, and then the wings folded back. Scatterwings sniffled and blotted her eyes on the back of both left wrists. "She is?"

"Yes."

"Do you know where she is?"

"Um." Nurk rubbed the back of his neck. "Um. Um."

This was getting worse and worse. "I . . . think she's . . . um . . . dead."

Scatterwings stared at him in disbelief. "Don't be stupid."

"Well, nobody's seen her in forever, so we just assumed—"

The dragonfly brushed this aside with a wave of multiple hands. "So you don't know where she is."

"No, like I said, we think she's—"

"Yes, yes, I heard." Scatterwings propped her chin on her palm, obviously thinking.

Nurk felt a little put out. The princess was not behaving like someone who had just learned that an old family friend had died; she was acting like he was an idiot. Nurk did not particularly appreciate that.

Scatterwings dropped her hand and looked him over from nose to tail tip. She did not seem particularly pleased with what she saw. Nurk felt his ears grow hot.

"Have you ever done anything heroic?" She didn't sound hopeful.

Nurk rubbed the back of his neck. "Well . . . not really."

"But you are Surka's grandson." She frowned. "Well . . . maybe that'll count for something. It's not like anybody *else* is doing anything."

"Is doing anything about what?"

Scatterwings waved a hand. "We'll talk about it later. First we have to get this boat unstuck."

"But—"

She beat her wings a few times and pronounced herself ready to go aloft.

"But—"

Nurk realized, as she began clambering up the mast, that he wasn't going to get any more information out of her.

"Good luck!" he called, as the dragonfly princess climbed up the mast. She bounced on the tips of her purple-painted toes and nodded down at him.

"I'll be fine. You just sit tight, and I'll be back with help in no time."

And with that, she launched herself into the air. Her wings beat so rapidly, they were a blur of bright color behind her. She shot upward, turning to a dark speck, and then was gone.

NURK SAT AND waited.

He sat and waited some more.

He continued to wait.

After about an hour of this, he started to get worried. Scatterwings had been very nice but possibly a little scatter*brained,* and she had been very disappointed that Surka wasn't coming. He scanned the sky for the hundredth time, but the sky was blue and empty of anything but clouds.

"I hope she doesn't get distracted by any shiny objects," he muttered to himself, and felt immediately unkind for doing so.

He tried to amuse himself by carving a small bit of wood into a dragon, but all he had to carve with were his scissors, so the dragon came out looking a bit like a seal. He tossed it overboard after a few minutes. It bobbed away.

The sky continued to be empty.

He got out the diary. With much patience and using a bit of scratch paper, he managed to translate three-quarters of an epic battle between Surka and a troll named Lumpy Frogsnuggler. Unfortunately, just as his grandmother had climbed on the troll's head and was clinging to its horns while it bucked wildly, her pen had begun to leak ink. The next few pages were even harder to read than usual, interspersed with large black blobs, and by the time Surka had bought a new pen, she was on a pirate ship headed for the Barbary Coast.

"I suppose she must have won," Nurk said aloud, "since the trolls made her their chief at some point."

He scanned the sky again. It was still empty—no, wait, there was a tiny black dot far in the distance. A bird? Another dragonfly? An inexplicably airborne turnip?

It was Scatterwings. She spiraled downward like a leaf and landed on the top of the Snailboat. The back draft from her wings made the sail billow, and the Snailboat creaked against the log.

"They'll be here any minute!" she reported happily.

Nurk searched the sky, looking for more black specks, but none were apparent. "Errr . . . who'll be here?" he asked, after a few minutes had crept by.

"The dragonfly nymphs," said Scatterwings, as if surprised he had to ask.

"What's a dragonfly nymph?"

"One of our people who live in the water instead of the air," said Scatterwings, and pointed. "There!"

Unfortunately, she pointed with both sets of arms, and in opposite directions, so Nurk turned around in place twice, trying to figure out what she was pointing at. At last he spotted a pair of ripples that seemed to be coming toward the Snailboat.

Two heads broke the water on opposite sides of the Snailboat's prow. Nurk squeaked.

The dragonfly nymphs were both much larger than Scatterwings and thus much larger than Nurk. They had the same reptilian faces as the dragonfly princess, although their eyes were liquid green and gold, and their throats and bellies were brilliant orange, more like newts

than dragons. Instead of the dragonfly's wild halo of hair, the nymphs had great fluttering manes of gills. They also had four arms, but the fingers were broad and webbed. Nurk glanced stealthily from hand to hand, but none of them had purple nail polish.

One of the nymphs put both right hands on the prow and smiled up at Nurk. "Is this your ship?" he asked.

Nurk's whiskers curled with pride at the Snailboat being called a ship. "Yes, it is!"

"It's a sweet little craft," said the nymph, bobbing his head. Nurk's whiskers practically tied themselves in knots. "We'll see what we can do to get it unstuck."

He ducked under the water again.

"They seem nice," said Nurk to Scatterwings.

Scatterwings nodded vigorously.

A few minutes later, the nymphs reappeared, frowning. They shook their heavy heads, and drops of water flew from their gills like jewels.

"The ship is stuck tight underneath," the first one said.

"We can't back it up—there are too many branches in the way," said the second one. "We might knock a hole in the bottom, and that won't do at all."

"It's not stuck forever, is it?" asked Nurk, horrified.

The nymphs grinned. "Naw," said one, patting the hull of the Snailboat as if to reassure the little ship. "We'll just need a little more help is all."

"We'll be right back," the second nymph assured

them. "Princess." He saluted Scatterwings with two fingers across his forehead. The other one followed suit, and they both dived and swam away.

Nurk tried to be reassured, but it wasn't easy. Anxiety felt like a small, nervous animal climbing around inside his chest. He paced back and forth, the few steps one could pace in a snail shell.

"Stop that," ordered Scatterwings.

"I'm nervous!"

"Some hero you are. You're going to wear a hole in the bottom, and then we'll sink."

"I doubt it," grumbled Nurk, but he sat down, anyway. Being called a hero gave him something else to worry about.

What if Scatterwings expected him to do something noble? The letter had been a call for help—what if she was expecting Nurk to help her?

He felt queasy. The thought of doing something heroic was terrifying, and the thought of having Scatterwings cry again was even worse. He wanted to ask her what she expected him to do, but he didn't quite dare.

"Look," said Scatterwings. "I brought a deck of cards. Let's play something."

They played a couple of hands of old maid, during which Nurk kept staring in the direction the nymphs had gone, until Scatterwings threatened to dump him in the river if he didn't hurry up and draw a card.

"Sorry," muttered Nurk. "Um, go fish."

"We're playing old maid."

"Oh, right." He stared at his cards. They seemed vastly unimportant.

"Oh, never mind—look there!" cried Scatterwings, throwing down her hand of cards. Nurk looked up again.

Now there were even more black specks in the sky— ten or twenty of them, a whole swarm. As they came closer, they were no longer black but green and gold and orange, and then they were dragonflies. The smallest of them was twice the size of Scatterwings, with huge, buzzing wings.

"Princess!" the leader cried, and all of them saluted Scatterwings in unison, who tossed her head and pretended not to care, then snuck a look at Nurk to see if he'd noticed.

Nurk was tongue-tied. He didn't know if he should introduce himself to the leader of the dragonflies, who was every shade of gold and orange imaginable, or sit quietly and hope nobody noticed him at all.

"Is that the king?" he whispered.

Scatterwings snorted. "No. That's just Amberskeins. He's the Captain of the Guard."

Several of the biggest dragonflies were carrying ropes of thin spider silk slung over their shoulders. At Amberskeins's direction, they uncoiled them and dropped them into the water. Nurk looked over and saw the nymphs had returned and had brought even more of their kind with them. Six nymphs grabbed the ropes and dived under the Snailboat. A moment later they emerged on the other side and handed the ropes up to hovering dragonflies.

Nurk was mystified. "What are they doing?" he asked.

"I'm not sure," Scatterwings admitted. "But the nymphs usually know what they're doing when it comes to boats and water."

Suddenly the Snailboat shuddered, as if something enormous had struck it from under the water. Nurk and Scatterwings both squealed and clutched at each other to keep from falling over. There was a splashing from below, and they could hear one of the nymphs laughing.

"Careful!" cried the nymph. "There's passengers on board!"

"Oh-oh-oh?" replied a deep, watery voice.

Nurk peered over the edge, and his eyes went very wide. Travel broadened the mind, but he hadn't known his mind could get *this* broad.

The owner of the voice was an immense carp, his head lifting just clear of the surface of the water. He was three times the size of the Snailboat, scales glistening milky white, with a broad red patch across the surface of his head. As Nurk watched, the great carp fanned his fins lazily and turned his head so that one round eye looked up at Nurk.

"Oho!" said the carp. "A shrew, is it? Is this your ship, little shrew?"

"Yes, Mister Carp," said Nurk, feeling that it would be a very good idea to be polite to the giant fish. (Ordinarily, he might have objected to being called "little shrew," but compared to the fish, anything short of a live cow would probably be little.)

"Then I shall be very careful," said the fish. He slid back down into the water and thumped one of the dragonfly nymphs with a huge fin. "*Mister* Carp!" he whispered, highly delighted. Even his whisper was a booming baritone that could probably be heard halfway back to Nurk's tree.

"Yes, yes," said the dragonfly nymph, rolling his eyes. "There'll be no living with you now . . ."

While Nurk and Scatterwings watched, and tried to stay out of the way, the operation was set. The ropes were tied off, and the carp dived under the Snailboat. The nymphs stationed themselves around the boat, and the dragonflies lined up overhead, three to a rope, gripping each line in both sets of powerful hands.

Nurk looked from rope to rope but couldn't see any purple nail polish on any of them. He was starting to think Scatterwings was just weird that way.

"On three," called Amberskeins. "One—two—THREE!"

The dragonflies heaved. The Snailboat shuddered and lifted halfway out of the water. Nurk and Scatterwings fell in a heap at the bottom of the boat, along with the deck of cards, the blanket, and Nurk's cooking pot.

There was a whumping, bumping noise from underwater, as the carp got his head under the Snailboat and pushed. The Snailboat rose even farther out of the water.

Nurk and Scatterwings tried to get untangled. This proved impossible, so then they just tried to get up. The dragonfly princess had cards stuck in her hair, and Nurk couldn't get the blanket unwrapped from his left foot, but they staggered to the prow together, anyway. This wasn't something either one wanted to miss.

It could not be said that the flight of the Snailboat was majestic. It was slow and awkward and moved in limping lurches, as the carp pushed and the dragonflies heaved and the nymphs steered it through the tangle of branches. But majestic or not, the Snailboat was coming free.

Nurk was delighted to see this and more than a little awed by the efforts of everyone involved. It seemed incredible to him that so many individuals could be working so hard, just because he'd fallen asleep in the Snailboat. He had no idea how he would make it up to them.

At last the dragonflies gave one last heave and the carp gave one last push, and the Snailboat slid over one last tangle and was free in the current once more. The nymphs cheered. Scatterwings whooped and danced around, shedding cards so wildly out of her mane that it looked as if she had developed a very unusual case of dandruff.

Before the boat could get swept back into the logjam, the great carp had the lead rope in his mouth and was pulling it out of danger.

"Thank you, Mister Carp!" Nurk called from the prow.

"Ymmf llkmm!" said the carp, through a mouthful of spider silk.

He pulled it in a broad circle, away from the logs, and in toward the western bank of the river. Where the water grew shallow, the carp relinquished the rope to the two burly nymphs, who hauled it in the rest of the way and tied the rope neatly up to a tree root.

Amberskeins landed on the root and, reaching down to the Snailboat, politely offered his arm to Scatterwings, who tossed her mane and said, "I can get out *myself*!" Which she did, with a few flicks of her bright wings and a lot of teenaged muttering.

Apparently unbothered by the princess's rudeness, Amberskeins reached several hands down to Nurk, who did appreciate the help. The shrew scrambled up the bank. "Where to now?" he asked the tall golden Captain of the Guard.

"Now," said Amberskeins, "we see the king."

CHAPTER SEVEN

"BEiNg IN cHARge isN'T mUCh FuN.
SuRe, YoU cAN sLeEP iN LAte, BuT THeRe
aRe So mAnY ThiNgs TO woRrY aBoUt aLL thE TiMe.
THe bEst PLaN FoR aNy sEnsibLE AdvEnTUreR iS to
sweeP iN, tAKe thE ThroNE, LivE Like a kiNG FoR a Few
wEeks, AnD thEn sNeAK oUT iN The MiDdLe Of thE
NiGht BeFoRe pEOpLE stARt asKinG UnPLeAsaNt
QuEstioNs aBouT RoAd mAinTEnaNcE
AnD tAx ReLieF."

THE KING OF DRAGONFLIES lived under a dog-rose
bush, in a large papery lodge rather like a wasp's
nest—but no wasp had ever had such a beautiful
door, of carved and polished wood set with panels of aba-
lone shell, and such soaring columns of rose stems twin-
ing around the walls of the palace; nor did any wasp ever
paint the papery sides with such elaborate decorations,
coils and spirals and shimmery swirls, in subtle tones of
white and gray and silver.

Other dragonfly dwellings hung at various heights

throughout the rose thicket, but they were much smaller and had simple doors with little projecting balconies to launch their owners into flight.

Nurk looked nervously around as Amberskeins led him into the corridor of rose stems leading to the palace. The passageway was cool and green and rustled with the movement of the rose leaves in the wind, but it also had wickedly curving thorns as thick as Nurk's arm. The shrew caught his tail up in his paws and carried it carefully out of the way of the whispering thorns.

Amberskeins paused before the door and turned to Nurk.

"Yes?" said Nurk, when the Captain of the Guard had looked down at him for a moment without saying anything.

"The king is not unkind," said Amberskeins slowly, "but he is very unhappy. We are all being . . . careful."

Nurk gulped.

"There is no danger," said Amberskeins hurriedly. "Only—be kind." And with that he struck the door with both left fists, and it swung open before him.

Me? Nurk thought. *Be kind to a king? Who am I to be* anything *to a king, kind or otherwise?*

The throne room was—well, it was really rather gloomy, Nurk thought. The papery walls let in light well enough, in a pattern of dappled light and green shadow, but it still seemed dark inside. If there were any lamps, they were unlit. Dragonfly warriors stood ringed around the walls, carrying needlelike spears, as quiet as four-armed statues. They glittered like cut gems even in the shadows.

At the far end of the room, in a backless throne framed by his enormous wings, sat the King of Dragonflies.

He was huge.

Easily half again as big as Amberskeins, probably three times the size of Nurk, the king was every color of the rainbow, with a few shades extracted from shellfish for good measure. Even in the gloom, his mane blazed scarlet and violet and gold, and his skin, the same sea-foam green as Scatterwings's, gleamed like mother-of-pearl.

His eyes were huge and fiery gold, and surely it was only the darkness of the room that made those eyes seem shadowed.

"Go forward and address him," murmured Amberskeins, and gave Nurk a little push between the shoulder blades when it became obvious the shrew would not be moving on his own.

Nurk walked unsteadily across the room. How close should he go to the king? Was he supposed to kneel or bow or salute? He wished Scatterwings were here, but she had flitted off as soon as the Snailboat had docked.

There were lines drawn on the floor, in colored earth, and he looked at them to make sure he was walking straight. He was concentrating so carefully on not drifting to one side or the other that he didn't realize how close he was to the throne until the king cleared his throat.

Nurk looked up with a squeak. He was nearly at the king's feet.

The King of Dragonflies looked at him with those huge, shadowed, golden eyes.

"I—um—hi—Your Majesty—?" said Nurk, and made a small, careful shrew bow.

"Hello, shrew," said the king. His voice was deep but quiet. It sounded like water running underground. "Your boat has been freed, has it not?"

"Yes, sir. Thank you very much, sir." Nurk clasped his paws together nervously. "Be kind," Amberskeins had said. "I don't know what I can do to repay you for your help. It was very nice of you. Um. Very, very nice of you. Wonderful. Um. Very nice. Um. Yes."

He stopped. There was probably a line between being kind and babbling, and Nurk was afraid he'd crossed it a few *um*s back.

The king studied him for a few minutes. The silence grew heavy and awful, and Nurk tried not to fidget.

"Are you brave, shrew?" asked the king, finally.

Nurk had no idea how to answer this question. It wasn't something he'd ever been asked. He thought desperately for some particularly brave moment from his past to hold up as an example but finally settled on the truth. "I don't know, sir."

"That is a fair answer," said the king, and lapsed into that heavy silence again.

Nurk wasn't sure if he was supposed to leave, or stay,

or do anything at all. He twisted his tail nervously in his paws and looked at the floor. It was rather pretty and had small stones set in it. He tapped one of his toenails against a stone. It was a stone, all right. He wondered what he should do next.

"There is something I would like you to do," said the king.

"Yes, sir?" asked Nurk, looking up hopefully.

"It is dangerous," said the king.

At this point, Nurk felt any danger might be preferable to the crushing weight of the king's silence and the gaze of those gold eyes. "Yes?" he said.

"My son, the Prince of Dragonflies, has been captured by the Grizzlemole," said the king.

This statement meant very little to Nurk. "I see. Errr, what's a Grizzlemole, sir?"

"A blind mole the size of half a mountain. He lives underground and is a powerful enchanter and a creator of terrible things. And when my son strayed into his territory on an errant wind, the Grizzlemole took him prisoner."

"He's *awful*," said Scatterwings from behind Nurk, making the shrew jump with a squeak.

Wonderful, Nurk thought, trying to smooth his fur down. *That should certainly convince the king that I'm brave.*

Scatterwings grinned at Nurk, then skipped up to her father. One of the large green hands that gripped the arm of the throne loosened, reached out, and stroked the princess's hair.

"Daughter," said the king. "It was well done to help this shrew."

"I couldn't just *leave* him," she said, tossing her mane. "He was *stuck*."

Nurk felt that this omitted a few key details, like Scatterwings being waterlogged and clinging to the branches, but thought it wouldn't be polite to mention it in front of the king. *Be kind,* he told himself. Whether being kind included Scatterwings as well as the king, he wasn't sure, but he figured better safe than sorry.

"Besides—," Scatterwings said, more quietly, "I wanted to rescue *somebody*."

This seemed like an odd thing to say, but the king reached out with both left arms and pulled her close. Nurk looked down at his feet again.

"You were telling him about Flicker?" asked Scatterwings.

"Yes." The king turned back to Nurk. "My son, Prince Flicker, is being held by the Grizzlemole in his lair."

"Why would the Grizzlemole do that?" asked Nurk.

The King of Dragonflies sighed. His brilliant hair waved and wavered like windblown grass on a hillside, if grass ever came in such blinding gemstone colors. "The moles are creatures of Earth," he said, "of deep places and darkness. And we dragonflies are creatures of air and light and open sky. We've never been friends, really, since the world began, but mostly we stayed out of one another's way. There have been some noble moles whom my ancestors were proud to know.

"But the Grizzlemole—the Grizzlemole is old and wicked, and he hates the sky and the glare of the sun. And he hates us for being flighty, frivolous creatures of air and sunshine. I don't think he planned to take my son, but once he had him, he saw no reason to give him up, either."

"I'm sorry," said Nurk. "You must miss him very much." No wonder the king looked so sad, the shrew thought.

"I feel like my heart is hollow," said the King of Dragonflies, "and the wind blows straight through it. It is very hard. But I hope—with your help—to get him back."

"*My* help?" squeaked Nurk, standing up very straight. "But what can I do, sir? I'm—I'm a shrew—I'm small—" It seemed very strange to him that the enormous king, who blazed like a sunset in the dark throne room, and all the powerful dragonfly warriors of his court, any one of whom could have knocked Nurk tail over teakettle with a flick of his wrist, could possibly think that a shrew could help them.

"Exactly," said the king. "The Grizzlemole has guarded his lair with strange magic, and he keeps close watch for dragonflies. No creature can get anywhere near his den by the air. If I or my warriors—and many of my warriors tried!—fly in, terrible winds come up and blow us in all directions."

Scatterwings coughed.

"In fact, unless I miss my guess, when you found her, my daughter Scatterwings had tried to fly to the rescue herself and gotten blown clear into the river!" said the king, glaring sternly at Scatterwings.

The princess blushed a kind of mottled bronze color and stared at her purple-painted toes. She mumbled something, which Nurk didn't quite hear and thought he was probably better off not knowing.

Now I know why she wanted to rescue somebody, thought Nurk. *Poor Scatterwings. She can't help her brother, so she helped me instead.*

"None of us can get there," said the king, turning back to Nurk. "No dragonfly, nor any of our friends who fly. The dragonfly nymphs would go, but they can only be out of water for a few moments at a time, and the Grizzlemole is likely to be watching for them as well. But a shrew—a shrew who comes by water, by the Snailboat—I don't think the Grizzlemole is watching for anything like that. I don't think he'd even notice you, if you were quick and quiet."

"Oh," said Nurk.

"*Please* say you'll go," said Scatterwings.

"Hush," said the king to his daughter. "That is unfair. It is a dangerous thing we are asking, young shrew, and you do not have to go. There is no obligation on you. We would have helped anyone stranded on our shores—this is not a debt we are asking you to repay, but a great favor that we ask of you. There is no shame in saying no."

"But he's Surka's grandson!" cried Scatterwings. "Surka always said she'd help us, if we ever needed it—"

"He is not his grandmother," said the king. "Her promises do not bind him."

Nurk wrung his paws together. He knew this was the adventure he had been looking for—what else could it be?—but now that it was put in front of him, it sounded terrifying. A mole as big as half a mountain! A wicked enchanter to boot! What was he, a shrew with the Snailboat and not much else, to do against such a creature?

His grandmother had been only a shrew, as well, but—well, the king had said it. He wasn't his grandmother. What could he possibly do?

"The Grizzlemole sleeps during the day," said the King of Dragonflies, as if reading his mind. "He does not like the sunlight. If you go early in the morning, you may be able to sneak in and out again without waking him. I would not ask you to fight the Grizzlemole yourself. He is too much for any shrew or dragonfly or dragonfly nymph."

Nurk gulped. Being kind was one thing, but this went well beyond kindness. He wanted, very, very much, to say that he was sorry, but he just couldn't do it.

But he thought of the portrait of his grandmother Surka, hanging in his hallway, and of the fierce shrew in her diary, wrestling trolls and setting out in search of monsters, and he knew she would have said yes.

And he'd opened the letter. The hummingbird had warned him. Maybe this was the price he had to pay.

It seemed awfully high.

He looked up. Scatterwings was watching him, her eyes shining a little too much, and he knew that if he said no, she'd cry.

And besides, said a little voice in the back of his head, *they know Surka, and they don't think she's dead. What if your grandmother's alive? If you help them, maybe they can help you find her.*

"Okay," he said, and was proud that his voice shook only a little. "Okay, I'll try."

"Oh, *thank* you!" cried Scatterwings, and flung both pairs of arms around him. Nurk found himself growing rapidly short on air and was very glad when the king said, "That's enough, daughter. He can't rescue Flicker if you smother him."

Scatterwings let him go, but then the great king himself was rising from the backless throne and bending down, until Nurk's vision was full of immense gold eyes and that rustling rainbow mane. The king reached out and clasped Nurk's paw in his own enormous green hands. His eyes were still sad, but there was a glimmer of hope far down inside them, too.

"Thank you, young shrew. May the luck of the dragonflies go with you."

———

NURK SPENT THE EVENING at the dragonfly palace in a guest lodge. It was nice to have a pillow again and a real bed instead of the floor of the Snailboat, but he had a hard time enjoying it. His dreams were full of enormous moles with blind white eyes, tearing down mountains with their great swordlike claws. By the time he woke up, his fur was damp with sweat, and he'd twisted the blankets into a crumpled mess at the foot of the bed.

A blue-winged dragonfly with a shuttered lantern came to wake him up and took him down to the root dock.

Scatterwings and the Captain of the Guard had come to see him off.

"I was hoping Surka would get my letter," said the dragonfly princess, "but you're her grandson, and that should be worth something."

Nurk nodded glumly.

"And if you get caught, I'll send another letter, and maybe she can rescue you both!" Scatterwings beamed at him.

Nurk nodded even more glumly. Tact did not seem to be one of Scatterwings's strong suits.

"I could paint your nails before you go," she said wistfully. "Then if you get scared, you could look at them and remember me."

Nurk suspected that if his nails were painted Gorgeous Grape, looking at them would only scare him worse, but it didn't seem to be the polite thing to say. "I don't think I have time," he said, instead.

"Maybe just one toenail?" she asked.

Nurk realized that Scatterwings really wanted to help somehow and couldn't think of any other way. "All right," he said. "*One* toenail."

She squealed with delight and pulled out her nail polish. Nurk sighed and took off one of his socks.

He didn't really want to watch the process, so he settled for looking at Amberskeins, who was carefully not watching Nurk and the princess. The Captain of the Guard's lips were twitching in a manner that made Nurk think he was probably fighting back a grin. The shrew sighed again.

"There! Perfect!" Scatterwings blew on his toenail. Nurk examined it resignedly.

"It's . . . um . . . purple all right," he said.

She hugged him with both sets of arms. "I hope it helps. Come back safe, and find Flicker!"

Amberskeins took the lead rope on the Snailboat and, taking to the air, hauled it away from the dock. A burly dragonfly nymph took charge of the rope and began hauling the Snailboat out toward the current.

"Good luck, young shrew," said Amberskeins, hovering over Nurk's head. Nurk nodded. From the shore, Scatterwings waved furiously.

"I'll do my best," he told the Captain of the Guard.

When the Snailboat reached the current, the nymph

handed the rope up to Nurk and waved. Nurk watched the heavy gilled head duck below the water, which rippled as the nymph swam away.

He was alone again.

Nurk dug out his grandmother's diary and found a page near the back.

ThEre Are FifTeeN oF Us, WeLl aRmEd fOR AnYThinG ThAt WilI coME oUR wAy. i hAvE a New sWORd aNd sHieLd AnD THe FinEst ARmoR, mAde FoR mE bY ThE bATTLe-hAmsTeR bLacksMiThs. gRoHgER SQuEAkinGdeATh kEePs cHEWinG oN His sHiELd. ThE oTheR hAmsTeRs ThiNk hE iS a beRSerkEr, bUt I Think hE is jUst wEiRD AnD NEeDs to bAthE moRe oFTeN.

He propped his feet up on the rim of the snail shell. The breeze slipped between his toes, drying the Gorgeous Grape. He wished he had a sword made by battle hamsters, although he didn't have the faintest idea of how to use one. Still, it would have made him feel a bit more prepared.

"I'm going into terrible danger to rescue a prince I've never met, and all I've got is a snail shell, clean socks, and one purple toenail," he said. "If this isn't an adventure, I don't know what is."

CHAPTER EIGHT

❻

"oH mY goD! iT's thE hiDeoUs sPiNe-cResTEd
AciD-dROoLiNg BeAst oF The NEtheRmoST MiREs!
AnD iT's coMiNg This WaY! NeaT!"

I T WAS NEARLY AN HOUR of sailing through undistin-
guished countryside before Nurk reached an area that
he could say was definitely not right. It looked like
a forest, but it was flooded in some fashion. The trees
came right down into the water, on thick, twisty roots,
like hundreds of fat legs, and the tops of broken logs stuck
out everywhere. He had to pull out the ginkgo oars to
steer between them.

For a few minutes, he'd been seeing things out of the
corner of his eye, things that looked like birds but weren't
quite right, but they always flew away before he could get
a good look at them. He figured it might just be nerves.

But the river began to get quieter and quieter, and the
mist, which had mostly burned off earlier, still clung on
this section of river, growing denser and denser the farther he traveled, until it seemed to be piling up like gauze

on either side of the Snailboat. The sounds of birds and insects faded, and there was only the slap of water and the soft creak of the Snailboat in the wind.

He saw another one of the strange birds, and this time it didn't fly away. It was perched on the stump of a dead tree jutting up from the water. Nurk looked at it, and then wished he hadn't.

The bird looked—more or less—like a heron. It had the tall, stiltlike legs and the long, snaky neck of a heron. But the ends of its wings had small babyish hands, and the beak—in fact, the entire face—looked false and artificial. Nurk stared, then realized it was a mask, painted to look like a heron. But if the creature *was* a heron—and with that neck and those legs, what else could it be?—why was it wearing a heron mask?

Nurk wondered what was under the mask and decided immediately that he really, really didn't want to know.

That must be one of the Grizzlemole's guards, he thought. *But I'm not a dragonfly.* "I'm just a shrew, just an ordinary shrew, no reason to stop me . . . ," he whispered to himself, hoping that if he said it often enough, it would be true.

He wondered if his grandmother, wherever she was, had ever claimed to be just an ordinary shrew.

The mask turned to follow his progress down the river. Dark eyes gleamed behind the eyeholes. Nurk swallowed hard and was very glad when the water carried him past the masked heron and farther into the trees.

BEING GLAD DIDN'T LAST very long. Nurk was scared. He didn't like this place one bit. Even though it was midday, it was dark and gloomy under the trees, and the yellow leaves that fell in the water swirled by like dim little stars.

He wished Scatterwings were here, nail polish and all.

He strained his eyes and whiskers to see in the dark ahead of him, and then he wished he hadn't. What looked like three large frowning faces stared back at him from the darkness. Nurk gripped the edge of the Snailboat with nervous paws.

The faces were lined up ahead of him, a little to the left of the Snailboat's course. They had dark holes for eyes, and their expressions were angry and sad. Nurk didn't know whether to grab an oar to fend them off or hide under the blankets until they went away.

The Snailboat drew closer and closer, and still the angry, sad expressions didn't change.

And then with a soft *plop!* one of the faces tilted and slipped into the water. The others followed. *Plop! Plop!*

"Travel broadens the mind," Nurk whispered to himself desperately. "Travel broadens the mind." He would not, not, not think of being attacked by severed heads. He wouldn't. "Travel—*eep!*"

On the last word, a wet, beaked head had risen from the water right next to the Snailboat.

It was a small black turtle, smaller than Nurk, with a pattern of orange on its shell that, in the gloom, Nurk had taken for a face. The shrew looked around and saw two other small turtles, wet and black and glistening, swimming around the Snailboat.

"H-hel-lo?" quavered Nurk.

The little turtles looked at him with their big, dark eyes, saying nothing, and then one by one they dived into the dark water and were gone from sight.

Nurk twisted his tail in his paws. The Snailboat, caught in the dark current, sailed on.

WHEN THE RIVER FINALLY opened up, the banks sweeping back and sunlight glittering down, Nurk felt an intense relief. It was a short open stretch—he could see darkness crouched on every side—but it felt like a reprieve.

Unfortunately, when the river broadened, it also grew shallow and quick, the riverbed glittering with pebbles, and Nurk had to haul frantically on the oars to steer the Snailboat out of the current before it was dashed against the rocks. The sun struck bright sparks from the water and glared unhelpfully into Nurk's eyes.

"Oh—oh—come on, Snailboat!—oh!"

The wickedly gleaming pebbles scratched at the underside of the little ship, making hard skreeking sounds, but the little shrew had learned just enough about steering to maneuver the Snailboat out of the current and into the quieter water beside the dark banks of the river.

"Whew." He wiped his tail across his forehead.

The Snailboat drifted quietly along the bank. Nurk sagged against the oars.

He felt tired but surprisingly good. The shallows had been frightening, but it was a danger he understood, and he had overcome it all on his own. He felt older and tougher and more competent.

Scatterwings would probably have laughed until she choked.

Still, his arms ached from pulling on the oars, and he looked around for a place to rest.

There was a large rock near the riverbank. Nurk turned his back and started to row toward it, and then something struck him, and he turned back, the oars held high and dripping.

"There's something not right about that rock," he said out loud.

It was broad and dark and rounded, just the sort of thing for pulling the Snailboat alongside safely, but for some reason—something he couldn't put a claw on—he didn't quite trust it.

"Don't be ridiculous," said the rock, "it's a perfectly fine rock."

Nurk nearly dropped the oars.

"It's a great rock, in fact," was the rock's opinion. "You should come and look at it."

Nurk had seen some unusual things in the last two days, but he hadn't come so far that he was going to just accept the word of a talking rock. Besides, he was pretty sure that—

"Rocks don't talk," he said warily.

"I'm not talking," said the rock. "You've obviously gone crazy and are hearing voices."

While Nurk had been doubting his sanity a bit—particularly since he'd agreed to rescue the prince—he was fairly sure that there was quite a long distance between mildly foolhardy and hearing the landscape talk. He steered away from the rock, giving it a wide berth.

"I don't think I'm *that* crazy."

"Crazy people never do," said the rock matter-of-factly. "But it's easily proved. Just come over to the rock and see for yourself if it's talking. Then you'll know if you're crazy or not."

"You know," said Nurk, pulling on the oars despite his aching paws, "I think I'm willing to live without knowing. I'm sorry. I'm sure you're a very fine rock, though."

The Snailboat began to ease past the suspicious stone.

The rock was silent for a moment, and then said, rather grumpily, "Oh, you're a *shrew*, aren't you?"

"Yes," said Nurk, wondering what that had to do with anything.

"Shrews are always trouble," muttered the rock, and then the water began to roil around it. A broad, dark head rose out of the water, and Nurk looked into the glinting golden eyes of an enormous snapping turtle.

The little shrew fell back with a frightened squeak— the snapping turtle could have eaten him in one casual bite—but the Snailboat was already past and beginning to pick up speed as it caught the edges of the current.

"The other one was trouble, too," said the turtle, annoyed. It dropped its head down and blew bubbles. Water slopped against the deceptively rocklike shell.

"What other one?" asked Nurk. The trees were closing in again, and deep, shadowed water loomed ahead. "Another shrew?"

"The other one," called the turtle. "The old female with the sword"—and then the Snailboat swept around a curve of the river, and the turtle was gone.

It was a little time later that the boat slowed, and slowed further, coming around the bend into a small harbor, deeply shadowed, among the roots of the mangrove trees.

Nurk hardly noticed, mulling over the turtle's words. An old female shrew with a sword—it sounded like his grandmother.

Could she really still be alive? Could she have passed this way?

"It could have been anybody," he told himself. "There are other warrior shrews. Or it could have been Grandma Surka but a long time ago." A snapping turtle that size must be very old, and it hadn't said how long ago the troublesome shrew had passed by. The turtle might have encountered her seasons ago. After all, an encounter with his grandmother, she of the severed-head fame, was likely to stick in anybody's memory, probably for quite a long time.

"More hints," he said to himself, rather sadly, "but nobody knows anything for sure. And this really isn't the time to be—"

And then he saw movement overhead, and his mouth opened, but no words came out at all.

Hanging over the water, only a few feet away, was a tree full of fish.

The tree had leaves rather like a beech, but from each cluster, hanging from its tail like an apple might hang from a stem, was an enormous hook-jawed salmon, twice the size of the white carp, capable of swallowing the Snailboat in three bites and a half. The faintest blush of red touched the silvery back of each fish. Their eyes were large and shiny, and all of them were fixed on Nurk.

Nurk could think of nothing to say.

The biggest salmon rolled its eyes and snapped its underslung jaw and spoke.

"GO," it said.

"A-," said the next one.

"WAY," said a third one.

Nurk wanted, more than he had ever wanted anything in his life—more than he had ever wanted adventure or the Snailboat or hot oatmeal for breakfast—to turn the Snailboat around and do exactly as the salmon said.

But he didn't. He thought of his grandmother Surka, the fierce warrior shrew, and knew that she wouldn't have turned back. He thought of the sad King of Dragonflies and silly Scatterwings, who were depending on him. And no matter how much he wanted to go home, he knew the young dragonfly prince probably wanted to go home much, much worse. "I can't," he whispered to himself, and then, a little louder, to the fish, "I can't." His voice shook terribly, and he was afraid the fish would notice.

The biggest one snapped its jaw again.

"YOU."

"DON'T."

"BE-"

"LONG."

"HERE," the fish said, one after another.

Nurk nodded miserably. The fish were right. It just didn't matter that they were right.

He looked to the left and the right, and finally saw it—a little sheltered beach, hardly more than a muddy bank with a few more pebbles than usual, tucked behind two trees. Using one of his ginkgo oars, he steered the Snailboat in that direction.

The fish watched him, unblinking.

Finally Nurk leaped out, into water up to his waist, and beached the faithful Snailboat on the pebbly shore.

"This must be it," he said to himself, looking around. "At least I don't see where else it could be . . ." He dried himself off with his by now rather battered towel and put on clean socks. He packed his raincoat and a sandwich and the pair of scissors, and then, with a sigh, put his very last pair of socks into his knapsack, slung it over his shoulder, and looked around at the Snailboat.

It was much harder than he expected to leave the little ship behind.

He checked Surka's diary for any last advice.

I wAs aLoNe. My comRAdes hAd dEseRTed Me. BeFoRe mE wAs THe LAir oF OgGA-oRMaThoN, tHE gReAt sNaUGwEigHt. mY heART raCeD, bUt I sTeELeD mYseLF aNd sEt oUt.

Oddly, this made him feel better. He didn't have the faintest idea what a Snaugweight was, but despite fifty seasons and unknown miles between them, it felt a little as if his grandmother were beside him. They were both going into danger alone, but in a way, they were alone together.

Nurk steeled himself and set out.

He picked his way across the beach to the tree of fish and looked up at them for a few minutes.

"Why are you in a tree?" he asked finally. "Shouldn't you live in the water?"

The salmon made a shuddery, juddery motion with its jaw. Nurk jumped backward and realized after a moment that it was a fishy laugh.

"WE."

"AREN'T."

"RIPE."

"YET."

When he got home, Nurk thought, he was going to tell Aunt Wilhelmina that she didn't know the half of it.

CHAPTER NINE

⑥

"tHE wORLd is A veRy oDd PlAcE,
AnD nOT aLwAys iN a GooD waY."

WHEN NURK LEFT the beach behind—and with a last longing look at his trusty Snailboat—he found himself in a forest so deep and dark, it might as well have been nighttime. Pale white mushrooms rose over his head, the undersides ribbed with hundreds of fleshy gills that dripped globs of slimy spores down onto the forest floor. The ground squished underfoot, and every few steps he slid on wet, rotten leaves and had to catch himself with a squeak.

He hadn't gone very far into the forest at all—although more than far enough to wish that he was somewhere else!—when he began to hear a noise.

It was not a good noise.

It was a swallowing, smacking, gnarfing, gnorbling kind of noise.

It was an *eating* noise.

And it was getting louder, the farther Nurk went into the forest.

"I have to keep going," Nurk whispered to himself. "I have to keep going." His feet seemed to have stopped moving forward. "I have to keep going," he told them. His feet did not seem very keen on this idea. Nurk couldn't blame them.

"Surka would keep going," he told his feet. Shamed into it, his feet started moving again.

The eating noise got louder.

He took a half-dozen steps, then a half-dozen more.

The eating noise was *really* loud now.

Ahead of Nurk, the darkness of the forest seemed to collapse into absolute blackness. It took a moment for him to realize that it was an old metal drainpipe ahead of him, forming a tunnel in the woods. The eating noises were roaring out of it, so loud now that Nurk clutched his ears, trying to blot it out. It sounded like a hundred giants having a banquet all around him.

He hoped the menu didn't include shrew.

He gritted his teeth and stepped into the tunnel.

Even with his paws clamped over his ears, Nurk could hear every footstep ringing like a church bell. *BONNNNG! MunchmunchgobblesnorfBONNNGsnarfswallowmunch* . . .

He tried to say something encouraging to himself, but he couldn't hear himself think, let alone speak.

It was a strange thing. Even though each footstep continued to echo loudly inside the pipe, the farther he went, the quieter the eating noises got. Was he going away from whatever was eating so loudly? Had he somehow passed it in the tunnel? Was it behind him now?

He might have turned around to look, frightened at the thought of a monster eating behind him in the dark, but suddenly he could see sunlight up ahead. Not much but little patches, the size of coins, shining through the leaves. It was the first sunlight he had seen since entering the forest, and he was very glad to see it. He thought that maybe if he could only stand, for just a minute, in a shrew-sized patch of sun, maybe he wouldn't be so scared.

Nurk walked toward the sunlight, each footstep kicking up ringing echoes behind him.

At last, blinking, he stood on the edge of the pipe. The eating noises had faded down to the merest whisper, a tiny munchmunchgobblesnarf, no more alarming than the chirp of a cricket. Nurk looked around, baffled.

There, in the mouth of the pipe, a small green caterpillar no longer than the tip of Nurk's nose was sitting on a twig, devouring a small green leaf with great gusto. Every bite it took, the sound was carried into the metal drainpipe, where it echoed and rang down the length, coming out vastly magnified. The caterpillar had black eyespots with little lines at the corners that made it look as if it were smiling.

Nurk let out a huge sigh that he hadn't known he'd been holding and sat down at the edge of the pipe to compose himself.

"I was really scared of you," he told the caterpillar.

"Swallowsnarflegobblegobbleyum!" said the caterpillar, ignoring him.

"I guess it just goes to show," said Nurk, feeling light-headed with relief, "that nothing's ever as big and scary as you think it is! Maybe the Grizzlemole isn't the size of half a mountain, either. Maybe he's not much bigger than me—"

A drop of slime fell on the back of Nurk's neck.

He looked up.

Hanging in the trees over the path was a caterpillar as thick around as an oak sapling. It was the same brilliant green as the tiny caterpillar, but each smiling black eyespot was twice the size of the Snailboat, and it had moving, squidgy mouthparts bigger than Nurk himself. As Nurk watched in fascinated horror, the caterpillar reached out and pulled a whole branch toward its mouth and ate it, very, very quietly, tearing through the wood as easily as the little caterpillar was eating its leaf. A sticky green slime of sap drooled from its mouth and fell on the forest floor.

Slowly, with a feeling of being trapped in a nightmare, Nurk turned his head and saw, for many yards ahead, that the trees were full of the giant caterpillars. The sunlight was breaking through here and nowhere else because these monstrous bugs were eating the branches. Slime dripped and drizzled and oozed from the tree canopy in syrupy strands.

Nurk finally found his voice, but all he could think of to say was "Ewwwww."

It was the most revolting thing he had ever seen, even worse than the time he'd left a glass of milk in his room and forgotten it was there, and it grew five kinds of mold and ate the glass. That had been pretty disgusting, but it had only been the size of a glass of milk. The caterpillars were the size of cows.

And they were so *quiet.* Somehow that made it much worse. When something is eating a whole tree, it should make a lot of noise. This soft, business-like eating was awful. Nurk had a horrible feeling that if the caterpillars ate *him,* it would be just as quietly. It would hardly make a sound.

Except for all the shouting he'd be doing, of course.

"Well," he said, finally. "I don't look very much like a leaf, so they probably won't try to eat me. I suppose that only leaves the slime to worry about . . ." He rummaged in his knapsack and found his raincoat.

He had just pulled it on when the tiny caterpillar came to the end of its leaf.

It stuffed the last bit of green into its mouth, then looked around for another one. The shrub it was on had been stripped completely bare.

The little caterpillar twisted its head this way and that, still clinging to its twig, and then it began to wail, a thin, hungry, pouty little sound.

"Eeeeeoooohaaaauuuunhhh!"

Its wail was no bigger than the rest of it, but the quiet suddenly got deeper and more awful.

Nurk looked away from the wailing caterpillar and saw that the giant ones in the canopy had all stopped eating.

One by one, their enormous heads with the huge black eyespots turned in the direction of the little caterpillar—and him.

"Huunh-ungh-ungh-ungh-rreeeee!" cried the tiny caterpillar, hiccuping in distress.

One of the giant caterpillars doubled back on itself—amazing that anything that thick could bend like that—and reached for the tree trunk. It began slowly shinnying downward, body rippling with muscle.

If it comes down here, Nurk thought, *it's going to be right next to me, and it might think I look tasty, or it might think I'm bothering the little one, or—*

Nausea warred with terror. Terror won. Nurk reached into his backpack and fumbled out the last cheese sandwich. He tore off a small chunk of bread and cheese and dangled it in front of the crying caterpillar.

"Hunugh-ungh-ungh—mmmff!" It took a bite of the sandwich, then another larger bite. Nurk hastily pulled his fingers away as the caterpillar chewed through the crust.

It finished the bit of sandwich in seconds, but this time Nurk was ready. Before it could let out another wail, he stuck the entire sandwich on the twig, which poked through it like a giant toothpick. The tiny caterpillar burrowed into the food with happy munching sounds.

Nurk looked up and saw that the giants had gone back to eating, and the one that had been descending was back out on its branch.

He felt limp with relief. Even the prospect of walking under those chewing horrors was not as bad as having them come down to the ground near him.

The caterpillars ignored him completely as the shrew walked gingerly into the sunlight. Drops of slime pattered down, but his fur stayed dry, even if his whiskers twitched in disgust with every drop. He had to look carefully at the ground before placing each step, skirting whole pools and puddles of goo, while all around him the horrible soft eating noises went on and on and on.

Eventually Nurk left the caterpillars behind, and the forest closed in darkly around him again. He was almost glad to see the darkness again, since it meant no more caterpillars.

He stopped at a small puddle and took off his raincoat and cleaned it as well as he could in the water. The slime was even more disgusting than he'd imagined it would be, and Nurk had a pretty vivid imagination. But it would have been even worse to put the raincoat, all covered in slime, back in his knapsack, particularly when he'd probably need it again going the other way, so he gritted his teeth and scrubbed it with handfuls of sand and eventually stowed it away, damp but clean.

He kept walking.

A line of white showed up in the gloom, far in the

distance. By now, Nurk didn't know what else the Grizzlemole might possibly be keeping to protect his den, and he was so scared that he had almost stopped noticing he was scared and had begun to notice that he was tired and a bit hungry.

He couldn't do much about being scared, but he sat down on a root and had a drink of water, all the time puzzling over that distant line of white. It looked a little like a wall at the top, but it was dark and sort of stripy at the bottom.

"In this place it could be practically anything," he said to himself. "Maybe it's a herd of zebras."

It was not a herd of zebras.

He was still quite far away when he began to make out what it was—a wall made of tall interwoven mushrooms. The caps were huge and a slimy blue-green on top. The gills underneath were as white as bone, and the stems were long and thin and wrapped around and under and over one another like a nest of earthworms.

"They don't look as bad as the caterpillars," Nurk told himself, and was surprised to discover that he actually believed this. He suspected he might live the rest of his life without seeing *anything* as bad as the caterpillars.

The wall was fairly loosely woven, once he got up close, and there were plenty of places where a shrew might climb through to the other side. Nurk poked at one of the mushrooms, expecting it to be slimy, but it was actually cool and firm and damp, like a raw potato.

"Oh. Well, that's not so bad." He took a better grip on the mushroom and began to climb up to one of the gaps in the wall.

The stems trembled when he grabbed them, and there was an odd, mushy creak from overhead. He looked up, and the mushroom cap overhead swayed—creaked—and then dumped a vast quantity of sticky spores directly on Nurk's head.

He began sneezing uncontrollably. The spores were worse than pepper, worse than hay fever, worse than anything. He had never sneezed so hard in his life.

He sneezed until he fell over backward, and then he kept sneezing, until his throat was raw and his eyes were red and watery and his ears popped. If a monster had come along at that moment and scooped Nurk up to eat him, he couldn't have lifted a paw to stop it. All he could do was sneeze and sneeze and sneeze some more.

He didn't even have any tissues to wipe his nose with.

Finally—it seemed like hours later—the sneezes slowed. Nurk dragged himself to another puddle and put his entire head in it, trying to wash the awful spores from his whiskers.

He looked at his reflection in the puddle. His fur was wet and clumpy, and his eyes were red, and he looked thoroughly wretched. He sighed. "Travel broadens the mind," he told his reflection. His reflection sneezed at him.

Well. This was a problem. He probably couldn't sneeze

himself to death, but there was also no way to climb through the gap when all he could do was sneeze.

Nurk glared at the wall. The mushrooms swayed, looking deceptively harmless. Nurk knew a fungus couldn't laugh at him, but he couldn't shake the feeling they were doing it anyway. He rummaged through his backpack.

What he really needed was a way to protect his nose. If he could just keep the spores out of his nose and mouth, he probably wouldn't sneeze nearly so much.

He pulled out the pair of socks and stared at them.

His last pair of clean socks. The really nice pair, with the rainbow stripes, that his great-aunt had knit for him.

"Well," he said, with a sigh, "this is it. One sock for me, and one for the prince, and after this, if my feet get wet, I'll just have to live with it."

He pulled the beautiful rainbow sock over his whiskers and onto his nose.

He nearly fell over when he stood up. Having his whiskers mashed under the sock made him feel like he was stuck in a tiny little box. It was like his eyes and his whiskers were fighting with each other—he could *see* the whole clearing, but his whiskers insisted he was someplace very cramped indeed.

"There's no help for it," he said to himself, or tried to say. It came out "Mmmapghgghlfuhipfh!" through the sock. Still, Nurk knew what he meant. He stepped up to the wall and grabbed hold of the stalk of the nearest mushroom and began to climb.

The spores fell thick and fast around him, first from one mushroom, then another. They caked his fur with sticky white powder, until he looked like a shrew in a snowstorm, although not many shrews in snowstorms wear bright rainbow socks on their noses. His eyes got redder and redder and watered, and he felt miserable, but he didn't sneeze.

It seemed to take a lot longer to get through the mushroom wall than he expected. The air through the sock wasn't good, and as the spores caked the sock, it got hard to breathe. He started to get dizzy, and maybe that had something to do with the spores, too. He spent several minutes just sitting, clutching the edge of one of the turquoise caps, which was the size of his table at home, before he realized that he had stopped moving.

I've got to keep moving, he thought. *If I can get through the wall, the air will be okay on the other side. I've just got to keep moving.*

A few minutes later, with a nasty sinking feeling, Nurk realized he didn't know if he'd gotten through the gap yet. He was looking down the stems, but had he climbed through them? Was this the way forward or the way back? He couldn't remember, and without his whiskers, he got disoriented much more easily. The forest was identical on either side, and his head ached horribly.

His chest felt tight. He didn't dare take the sock off.

"I can't stay here," he muttered into the sock. "I have to go forward. If I wind up back where I started, I'll just have to start over, but I can't stop." He plunged forward, slipping and sliding down the stems, in a blizzard of spores, no longer sure if he was climbing or falling, but just wanting to be free of the horrible mushroom wall.

He seemed to have stopped moving. Nurk opened one eye and discovered that he was lying on the ground. He didn't think he could stand up, so he started to crawl, away from the spores, onto ground dark and damp with leaves and moss.

I still can't breathe, he thought. *Why can't I breathe?*

Because there's a sock on my nose.

He yanked the sock off and promptly sneezed. The sock was solid white with spores.

Covering his nose with one paw and sneezing weakly, he beat the sock against a tree root. White bits flew. Pale stripes started to show through the white. He whacked the sock on the root again and again, and the stripes got brighter and brighter as the spores came off. Unfortunately, they hung in the air like dust, and even with a paw over his nose, he started sneezing harder and harder.

He pulled the sock back on, and his sneezing subsided. Without the thick covering of spores, it was much easier to breathe through the fabric. He didn't want to think about the return trip through the wall. He just hoped the dragonfly prince would be able to make it.

Assuming I find the prince. Assuming I come back this way at all. Assuming the Grizzlemole doesn't lock me in a cage or eat me outright.

This line of thought was not productive.

Nurk started walking. Gradually, the cloud of white fell behind him. The forest didn't look familiar, so perhaps he'd gone the right way, after all. He went around a bend in the path and couldn't see the mushroom wall at all.

At the end of the path was a hole.

It was a very large hole, almost a cave, angling steeply down in the dirt. The edges were dry and crumbly, and bits of dead roots stuck out like grasping fingers. The discarded husks of dead beetles were scattered like cracked and hollow stones around the opening.

It's funny, Nurk thought. *An hour ago this would have scared me to death. But after the caterpillars and the mushrooms, it's just a hole, and there's nothing much scary about a hole, no matter what's at the bottom of it.*

Still, it was almost a ritual now. He reached into his backpack and pulled out his grandmother's diary.

WHeN bARGaiNiNG wiTh WiNd gYPsiEs, Be sURe to sPeAK eNTirelY in RhYmE. THeY CoNsiDeR rHYmiNg a SiGn oF hoNEstY AnD wiLL reFUsE a BaRgAin To oNe wHo CANNot RAtTLe OfF a qUick coUpLEt oR two.

Do NoT tRY to BuY oRAnGeS FRom wiND gYPsiEs.

Probably good advice, Nurk thought. Not at all relevant to the situation at hand, but probably good advice.

He straightened his shoulders and drew himself up to his full, inconsequential height and went to find the prince.

CHAPTER TEN

⑥

"a tRUe aDvEnTuReR nEeDs a keeN WiT,
a sTOut HeARt, aNd a stRONG bLAdDeR.
DuMb LUck cAn stAnD in FoR thE WiT aNd THe heARt,
bUT i'vE NEveR yEt FouND a GOod sUBstiTutE
foR thE BLaDdER."

THE HOLE GOT VERY DARK, very fast. The light from outside died out after the first bend, and Nurk stumbled along in the dark, with one paw on the wall. He hoped there weren't any gaping pits or poisonous snakes. It didn't seem sensible for the Grizzlemole to litter his front hallway with pits or snakes, but anybody who kept giant caterpillars and walls of mushrooms probably wasn't dealing with reality as Nurk knew it, anyway.

There was a faint, rhythmic whistling noise in the tunnel. Nurk wasn't sure if it was just the movement of air or something more sinister, but it rose and fell in a regular pattern around him.

After what seemed like a very long time, Nurk saw a flicker of orange far off in the distance.

It was a reflection of firelight on a bit of shiny pebble. Nurk reached out and touched it in relief, then turned. The tunnel, painted in faint red light, made a switchback turn and seemed to open up at the end. The whistling noise was louder now, and at the end of each whistle was a bubbling noise.

Nurk was getting a bad feeling about that whistle.

Moving as quietly as he could, cringing whenever sand crunched under his toes, the shrew slunk to the tunnel mouth and looked out.

The cavern was large, with a hollowed-out fire pit. The fire was banked down to coals, but the dim red light was more than enough to illuminate the face of the sleeping Grizzlemole.

Nurk whimpered soundlessly.

The Grizzlemole was the size of half a mountain, and he was hideous. When the King of Dragonflies had called him a mole, Nurk had thought of one of the little gray scuffling moles, with pointed snouts and thick grubby claws. He had not envisioned anything remotely like this.

The curve of the Grizzlemole's back went up practically to the ceiling in a great sweep like a steep hillside. Dirty white fur stuck out in clumps, and the claws were the size of plows and the gnarled yellow of old toenails.

The worst, though, was the nose.

The Grizzlemole had some kind of growth under his nose that resembled a giant fleshy mop. Instead of nostrils, there were dozens of thick, ropy tentacles, ridged

like the bodies of worms. Any one of the tentacles was longer than Nurk from nose to tail tip.

The source of the whistling noise was now obvious. As the Grizzlemole breathed, the air slithering through those lax tentacles made a shrill whistling snore.

As long as he's snoring, I'm safe, Nurk thought desperately. *As long as he's snoring, he's not awake.*

He looked up from the nest of tentacles and met the Grizzlemole's eye.

It was only his terror that kept Nurk nailed to the spot, as he stared into that half-lidded, milky gray eye.

He's looking at me, he's watching *me, he's* awake, *oh help—*

Wait.

Wait, the Grizzlemole is blind . . .

He realized, as the creature continued to snore, that he was sleeping with his eyes half open. Nurk shuddered and turned away.

On the far side of the cavern was a curious construction made of twisted tree roots. It looked more like a ball of loosely woven twine than a prison cell, with an equally knotted door, and yet Nurk could make out a slumped green form sitting in the bottom of it.

That must be the Prince of Dragonflies, he thought.

Nurk really, really, really did not want to walk across that cavern, with the great Grizzlemole snoring with his eyes open and those awful tentacles lying in a tangle across the floor. But what choice did he have? He gritted his teeth and took a step away from the tunnel, and then another.

Once he was a half-dozen steps from the wall, he felt so exposed that it was easy to keep going, in hopes of getting to a shadow and whatever questionable safety it might offer.

He fetched up against the root cage at last. Poking his nose through the twisted wooden bars, he could see the dragonfly sitting inside. There was a definite family resemblance to Scatterwings and the king, but this dragonfly was smaller than Nurk and looked thin and pale.

"Hssst!"

The prince's head jerked up, and he came immediately over to the side of the cage.

"What manner of creature are *you*?" he asked, staring at Nurk's nose.

Nurk realized that he had neglected to take off the sock. He pulled it quickly off his nose. "I'm a shrew!" he whispered. "Scatterwings and the King of Dragonflies sent me to rescue you!"

"You're an awfully scruffy-looking shrew," said the prince doubtfully. "How do I know my family sent you and this isn't some kind of trick of the Grizzlemole's?"

Nurk was stumped. It had honestly never occurred to him that the prince might not believe him. "Why would I trick you?"

"The Grizzlemole is cruel. It might amuse him to make me think I was being rescued and then dash my hopes."

"Oh. Oh dear." Nurk thought for a minute. "Oh!" He bent down and pulled off a sock.

"There!" Nurk hopped on one foot and wiggled his toes through the bars. "*Now* will you believe I know Scatterwings?"

"That's Gruesome Grape, all right," said Prince Flicker, studying his toe. "Can't argue with that."

"Then let's get out of here!" said Nurk. "Before the Grizzlemole wakes up."

"Easier said than done," said the dragonfly. "There's the small matter of me being in a cage."

"Oh." Nurk examined the cage closely. The root bars were thick and gnarled, in places bigger around than Nurk's arm. The only exit was the root door, and it was locked by an enormous padlock. "*Hmm.*" He looked in his backpack. His scissors were a good, sturdy pair and so would probably only take about a year to cut through the padlock. He could perhaps get through one of the tree roots in six months. He suspected that the Grizzlemole was going to wake up before then.

"There's a key," said Flicker. "On a cord around his neck. You have to get the key. Just don't touch the things on his nose. They're very, very sensitive. I think he uses them to see."

Nurk stared at him and then turned, very slowly, and looked at the Grizzlemole.

He was still a horrible mountain of flesh and fur, but now, looking carefully, Nurk could see a thin red cord running around the massive neck. Near the floor, almost lost in the shadow of those enormous sickle claws, was the faintest little gleam of what might be a key.

To reach it, Nurk would have to walk up to the Grizzlemole, step over that horrible tangled mass of tentacles, and stand inside the curved circle of claws. He would be directly in front of the Grizzlemole's left eye. If the creature so much as twitched a finger in his sleep, Nurk would barely have time to squeak before the Grizzlemole caught him and there would be two prisoners in the root cage.

"I don't think I can do it," said Nurk weakly.

"You have to!" said the dragonfly prince.

"I know I have to," said Nurk. "I just don't know if I *can*."

He stood by the edge of the cage for several minutes, holding the scissors. He knew he should try to talk himself into it, but his mind was an absolute blank. All he could see were those awful tentacles and the long, long claws.

"If you can't do it," said the Prince of Dragonflies, "then you should probably go back before the Grizzlemole wakes up."

That shook Nurk out of his stupor. To go all the way back, past the caterpillars and the mushroom wall, back to Scatterwings and her father, and have to say, "No, I was there; I just couldn't do the very last thing"—no, that was too much. He had to get the key.

With his tail looped firmly over one arm and his whiskers tucked in tightly against his nose, he walked slowly up to the Grizzlemole.

The tentacles were the worst. He had to decide where to put each foot before he took a step, so that he didn't so much as brush one. While he was doing this, he was directly in front of the Grizzlemole's nostril, and every time the monster let out one of those train-whistle snores, a blast of hot, wet air showered Nurk's fur.

He took another step. The next one carried him out of the snore radius and past the tentacles. The claws curved around behind him, a ribbed wall taller than Nurk's head.

He looked up at the Grizzlemole's eye.

The eyelid was still only half closed. The hairs were sparse around the eyelid, sprouting in coarse white clumps, with pale, dirty pink skin visible underneath. As the shrew watched, something small and white, with lots of legs, crawled across the eyelid and into the mole's fur.

Nurk felt sick.

He turned to the key. It was bigger than his paw and made of polished black iron. The red cord, which looked so small on the great curve of the Grizzlemole's back, was thicker than Nurk's wrist.

He had to use both paws to get the scissors to cut the twisted cord. He sawed at it, trying not to pull on the cord at all, cringing at every motion.

It seemed to take hours. It seemed to take seasons. It couldn't have been much later than noon when he entered the burrow, but Nurk felt that surely he had been working on this cord for much too long, that it was getting dark, and at any moment that tiny, wicked eye would open all the way, and the claws would flex, and the Grizzlemole would wake up.

The last thread began to part. Nurk quickly grabbed the key so that it wouldn't fall and finished cutting.

The key dropped silently into his paw. He exhaled.

Turning around in place without touching anything was actually the hardest part of the whole endeavor. But he managed, inch by inch, and picked his way out from between the tentacles.

He was nearly free and just starting to breathe easier when there was a horrible snorfling noise behind him, and the immense claws came down around him like a cage of swords.

Oh no oh no this is it he woke up I'm going to die . . .

Nurk stopped breathing. The claw looked like ancient ivory, a filthy yellow, shot through with fine cracks and splattered with dirt.

About half a minute slid by, and he started breathing again, because nothing else had happened, and, anyway, there is no terror that is made better by asphyxiation.

The claws didn't move. The snorfling noise settled back into a muttering snore.

Nurk turned his head, very, very slowly, and saw the Grizzlemole's tentacles twitching a bit, but no other motion.

He's still asleep. He just moved in his sleep. That's it. He didn't wake up. Nurk let his breath out. A damp circle of condensation appeared on the Grizzlemole's claw and then melted immediately away.

Unfortunately, even if the Grizzlemole was still asleep, Nurk was now trapped in a cage of claws. They were too close together for even a shrew to squeeze between. The Grizzlemole's immense palm, wrinkled and patched with wiry hair, arched over his head.

"Hurry!" hissed Prince Flicker from his cage.

Nurk didn't dare reply. He was too close to the Grizzlemole's ears.

I have to get out, he thought desperately. *He has to move again so I can get out!*

The Grizzlemole snored, looking about as likely to move as a mountain.

If I can make him move in his sleep again somehow—oh, but what if he closes his paw?

If he moves, I might be squished.

If he doesn't move, I'll definitely *be caught.*

Oh, what would Surka do?

He sighed. Surka would have run the Grizzlemole through with her gleaming sword or ridden the monster around the room using his tentacles for reins, but neither option was possible for him.

If I ever do this again, he thought tiredly, *I must remember to bring a gleaming sword. And perhaps learn how to use it.*

Still . . .

He glanced over at the tentacles thoughtfully.

He wasn't his grandmother, and reins were out, but still . . .

His nose is very sensitive, Flicker had said.

Nurk knelt down and leaned forward. He couldn't squeeze between the claws, but he could poke most of his nose through the gap between two of them.

"We'll find out how sensitive your nose really is," Nurk said under his breath.

The claws were as solid as stone, and they scraped uncomfortably against his cheeks, but Nurk wiggled and shifted and strained until his long white whiskers popped free of the cage.

He pressed himself flat on the floor, and by wiggling his nose determinedly, he managed to brush a whisker against one of the Grizzlemole's tentacles.

The tentacle didn't respond.

Nurk strained forward as far as he could and wiggled his nose furiously. He could feel the tip of his whisker going flick-flick-flick against the tentacle.

For a long moment, nothing happened. Nurk's ears sagged with doubt—would the Grizzlemole even notice? If he did notice, would he wake up?—and then the Grizzlemole grunted, the tentacle twitched, and the enormous claws lifted away.

The Grizzlemole swiped at his nose in a halfhearted scratch, mumbled a bit, and lapsed back into snores. The paw dropped back to his side.

Those immense claws would probably have cut Nurk in half when they landed, but as soon as the Grizzlemole had scratched his nose, Nurk had scrambled forward on all fours. Half crawling, half falling across the stone floor, he pulled himself free of the Grizzlemole's embrace.

For a minute all he could do was lay sprawled across the floor, panting. He felt pounded flat, like a shrew-skin rug. The iron key was a cold weight in his paw.

I did it, he thought. *I did it. I got the key. I did it.*

He got up. He couldn't believe he'd done it.

Nurk practically skipped to the cage to unlock the prince but restrained himself. There was no need to get weird.

The key fit smoothly into the lock, and Nurk opened the door with agonizing slowness, afraid of a creak or a squeal of metal. The prince was practically dancing with impatience on the other side, but Nurk didn't dare throw the door open and risk a noise that would betray them both.

But the door opened with no more than a quiet rattle of roots, and the dragonfly prince stepped out and clutched Nurk with both sets of arms.

Nurk bore the hug patiently—if he had been locked in a cage for that long, he'd have hugged his rescuer, too—and then began leading Prince Flicker across the floor, to the mouth of the tunnel.

Skreeeeeee-chunk!

The iron padlock, which had been dangling at an

awkward angle from the door, succumbed to gravity and slid free.

Flicker made a gulping sound of pure horror.

Slowly, slowly, as if in a nightmare, Nurk turned his head and saw that the Grizzlemole's blind eyes were fully open.

The monster was waking up.

CHAPTER ELEVEN

⑥

*"SOONER OR LATER YOU HAVE
TO STAND ON YOUR OWN TWO FEET, STARE DEATH
IN THE EYE, AND SAY, 'COME AND GET ME,
IF YOU'VE GOT THE GUTS!'"*

"WHO . . . IS . . . IN . . . my . . . cave?" whispered the monster, in a voice like dead leaves rustling underground.

The massive head lifted, and the tentacles began to move and wriggle, slowly at first, then more rapidly, until the ones on the fringes were whipping wildly about, striking the Grizzlemole's muzzle. The giant claws flexed and turned, as he set them against the earth.

He can't see us, Nurk thought frantically. *He's blind. He can't know where we are.*

"Do you . . . seeee . . . my tentacles?" hissed the Grizzlemole. "They . . . are . . . better than eyesss . . . in the dark . . ."

And to Nurk's profound horror, the Grizzlemole

began to grope this way and that with the terrible fleshy fingers under his nose, reaching out with them, sending them writhing over the floor and the walls and the root-covered cage, like an army of blind serpents.

"I don't . . . *have* . . . to . . . seeee you . . . ," breathed the mole. "I can . . . feel . . . your *thoughts* . . ."

The tentacles were coming closer. Prince Flicker was rigid beside him. Nurk tried to grip one of the dragonfly's wrists and discovered that he still held the iron key in his paw.

The closest tentacle crawled a whisker's width from Flicker's feet.

Nurk pulled his arm back and flung the key, as hard as he could, across the room. It hit the iron cage with a rattle of roots and fell down to the floor with a metallic clunk.

The Grizzlemole's head jerked up, and he whipped around toward the sound, the tentacles roiling and twitching at the end of his muzzle. Nurk grabbed Flicker and hauled him toward the hole. The dragonfly was deadweight for a heartbeat, and then he seemed to come to himself and began to run.

They fled up the burrow, toward the surface. Behind them the Grizzlemole shrieked.

"I feel you! I *feel* you, shrew!" The burrow shook as the Grizzlemole got his head and shoulders into it. Nurk darted a glance back and saw the great claws, like plows, digging into the dirt and pulling the huge body forward.

They ran.

The light died behind them as the Grizzlemole blocked the tunnel.

"I can't see where I'm going," moaned Flicker.

"Just keep running!" said Nurk.

They tried, but it's nearly impossible to run full tilt in the dark for very long, particularly when you're holding on to someone else, even if you're not exhausted and half sick with terror. Nurk ran with his whiskers straining and his arm brushing the side of the tunnel, trying not to run into the walls. But every turn and twist and patch of broken ground slowed them further. Behind them, the sliding, chuffing, tearing noise of the Grizzlemole coming up the tunnel grew nearer and nearer.

They had been reduced to a kind of stumbling jog when Nurk started to see things—shadows on deeper shadows, hints of motion. It took him a moment to realize that it was his own paw he was seeing, stretched out in front of him, and a moment more to realize that it was because there was daylight coming from up ahead.

"We're almost there!" he yelled, and pulled Flicker forward in a last brutal run.

Something thick and writhing and clotted with earth brushed his tail.

Another moment—another heartbeat—and it would

have been too late. But they broke from the mouth of the hole into light that seemed dazzlingly bright, even if it was no more than the dim light of a deep forest in the afternoon, and the Grizzlemole cringed backward with a hiss.

"Don't stop!" Nurk gasped. His chest felt like a cow was dancing on it, but he couldn't imagine that a creature like the Grizzlemole would be completely stopped by a little filtered sunlight.

And, indeed, they had gone only a few more steps when the sliding and chuffing began again behind them.

"It will take . . . more . . . than light . . . to save you . . ."

They kept running. If you run far enough, you're supposed to get your second wind. Nurk kept waiting for his and was desperately hoping he hadn't already passed it.

"Can you fly?" he said, panting, as they ran.

The dragonfly prince shook his head. "Harder than running," he said. "Too long . . . in . . . the cage."

They rounded a bend, and a band of white shimmered ahead of them. '

Nurk dropped the prince's arm and swung his knapsack around front, so that he could reach into it while running. It slowed him down, and he could hear the Grizzlemole gaining but not so quickly now. Maybe they could make it.

But if they were going to make it—

"Put this on your nose," said Nurk, pulling the rainbow socks out of his backpack.

It was astonishing, he thought, that even at a dead run, pursued by a gigantic monster out of some horrible primitive age, Flicker still found time to give him a look like he'd gone completely out of his mind.

"What?"

"Just put it *on*!" He hauled his own over his nose by way of comparison.

Clearly baffled, Flicker put the sock over his face. The rainbow stripes clashed badly with his hair. It would have been funny, if not for the bit with the running for their lives and the giant shrieking Grizzlemole behind them.

Let us get out of this, Nurk thought, as he flung himself forward into the wall of mushrooms. *Just let us get out of this, and I will never, ever ask for another adventure again. Ever.*

He started to climb. Behind him, panting through the sock, came the prince.

The dragonfly was obviously far better suited for climbing than Nurk was—he had an extra pair of arms and was using his wings for extra lift. He tried to help Nurk up, but the shrew waved him upward. "Go, go! Hurry!" he cried, although the sock turned it into "Gff! Gff! Rrrghheee!" Still, Flicker seemed to get the point and rapidly outdistanced him.

Spores began to drift down around them, whipped into eddies by the fanning of Flicker's wings. Nurk tried to breathe shallowly through the sock. Hauling himself along was twice as bad the second time around, although the dragonfly's passage had gouged handholds in the mushroom stems.

He looked down, just as the Grizzlemole reached the wall.

I have one chance at this, Nurk thought, *and it probably won't work, and I probably won't live through it—but what else can I do?*

He wished there were time to consult the diary. But there was no time left, and the situation was in his paws, and not his grandmother's or anyone else's. The letter sent to her had propelled him, and the diary had helped him, but it was all down to him now.

This was *his* adventure.

He closed his eyes briefly and prepared to meet his grandmother in the afterlife, somewhat sooner than he had anticipated.

"I . . . smellll . . . you . . . ," hissed the Grizzlemole. Nurk opened his eyes and watched the pink tentacles climbing up the white mushroom stems.

"Yes," said Nurk, his voice shaking horribly, "but I bet you can't *reach* me."

The Grizzlemole reared up on his hind legs. He was huge. His head was barely below Nurk's level. The shrew could have stepped off the mushrooms and walked down the monster's snout. This did not seem like a particularly good idea, but he could have.

Nurk found one of the gaps in the mushroom wall and braced himself against it. The tentacles slithered below him.

"Shrew?" called Flicker from the other side of the wall. "Shrew, are you okay?"

The Grizzlemole roared in frustration and took a great tearing swipe at the wall with his enormous claws.

Nurk flung himself backward into the gap, the claws passing barely a whisker's width from his body. Mushroom flesh sheared away in deep ruts, falling in chunks around the mole, and the whole wall buckled and shook.

Every mushroom cap along the wall seemed to vibrate together, as if screaming in some kind of fungal pain, and dropped their full load of spores, all at once.

If it had looked like a blizzard the first time Nurk had come through, this looked like a whiteout. He scraped the foul stuff out of his eyes, just in time to see the Grizzlemole fall backward in a cloud of spores, his tentacles so coated in white that he looked as if he'd been rolled in flour.

The Grizzlemole began to sneeze.

He had a surprisingly high-pitched, dainty sneeze. Nurk peered over the edge of the wall and saw the mole clutching at his face with his claws, while the tentacles writhed and snapped, caked in spores, and the monster sneezed and sneezed and sneezed.

Nurk could almost feel sorry for the Grizzlemole—having a nose that big and that sensitive and completely covered in spores. Well, he wasn't going to stick around to see how badly the mole suffered. He wriggled through the gap and half climbed, half fell down the other side.

Flicker was waiting for him. Arms around each other's shoulders, they staggered away from the mushroom wall, until the sneezes faded in the distance.

"The sock worked," croaked Flicker, pulling it off his face.

"Never go anywhere without clean socks," Nurk said.

The giant caterpillars were still munching quietly overhead. Nurk spread the raincoat over both of them, and they hurried down the slimy path. Flicker's wings got full of caterpillar drool, but there wasn't any help for it.

"At least they aren't trying to stop us," said the prince.

"Don't give them ideas," Nurk muttered.

They hurried into the metal pipe, past the tiny caterpillar happily munching on a new leaf, and down the pipe. The sounds of a giant's feast began to echo around them, but neither of them cared. They hurried on, slipping on the wet leaves, until they stumbled out onto the beach.

There, moving gently with the water, was Nurk's beloved Snailboat. He had never been so glad to see anything in his life.

Flicker climbed in and grabbed the oars. Nurk pushed the snail shell away from the shore, splashing alongside it—his socks were soaked, but he just didn't care anymore—and let the dragonfly haul him up once they were away from the beach.

The salmon in the tree noticed them and started rustling in agitation. They snapped their jaws and beat their fins against the air, then began shouting an alarm. They didn't seem very clear on which alarm to raise, so they tried all of them.

"FEAR!"

"FIRE!"

"FOES!"

"FLOOD!"

"FROGS!"

All the salmon glared at the last one, who flushed and tried to hide behind its leaves.

Prince Flicker dragged on the oars with both sets of arms, while Nurk scrambled up the Snailboat and raised the sail. They began to make slow progress against the current. The yells of the salmon receded behind them.

Nurk took a turn on the oars after a few minutes. The drowned forest crept by.

"I hope those fish don't alert anybody," said Flicker, peering back the way they had come.

The sail filled a bit more, and the Snailboat began to move slightly faster, although not nearly fast enough for Nurk's nerves. He started seeing things out of the corner of his eye again, and they seemed to be moving faster than before. Also, there seemed to be a lot more of them.

A soft splash came off to the right. Nurk looked up.

The masked heron-thing was walking toward them, with long, slow strides. Its little hands clenched and unclenched at the ends of its wings.

"What do we do?" asked Flicker.

"Row!" Nurk threw his back into the oars, and the Snailboat picked up speed, but so little, so little! The heron-thing was halfway to them now.

"Come *on,* Snailboat!" Nurk whispered. "Come on!"

The sail billowed as the breeze came up. The Snailboat shot forward on the water, and the heron-thing began to recede. Nurk and Flicker started to cheer.

Suddenly the creature took three long running strides and spread its wings. Nurk and Flicker stopped cheering.

The heron-thing's wing beats were slow and steady, and it closed the gap between them in barely any time at all. Nurk lifted an oar and prepared to sell his life dear.

The thing reached a hand up to its mask, as if to lift it and show them whatever awful thing lay beneath.

Flicker put his wings over his head.

Bzzzzzzzzzzzzzt!

A cry rent the air from many throats. "For the prince!"

Before Nurk's bewildered eyes, a dozen dragonfly warriors, in every shade, came sweeping out of the sky and rammed into the heron, knocking it sideways into the water. It staggered to its feet. They knocked it down again. Nurk could see Amberskeins in the lead, clinging to the top of the bird's head and whacking it vigorously between the eyes.

Mask askew, the bird-thing clearly had no more stomach for battle. Hunched like a vulture, it fled for the cover of the forest in a series of awkward lurches. Amberskeins leaped off just as it reached the trees.

A wet hand grabbed Nurk's wrist. Nurk squeaked and nearly whacked it with the oar.

"Careful, there!" cried the dragonfly nymph who had grabbed him. "Pull in your oars and strike the sail; we'll tow you in."

"Oh, thank you!" said Nurk, dropping the oar. He and Flicker hurried to roll up the sail. The dragonfly nymphs caught the lead ropes and began towing them swiftly through the water.

Amberskeins flew next to them. "Prince!" he cried, saluting. And, "Shrew! Well done!"

"You saved us," Nurk said. "Thank you! How did you know?"

"We didn't," said Amberskeins. "We were waiting just outside the Grizzlemole's territory, in case you got out and were hurt and needed help. The Snailboat just barely made it—a few inches less, and we couldn't have gotten in to help you."

"It's a good little ship," said one of the nymphs from the water.

Nurk patted the snail shell gratefully. "Yes, it is."

CHAPTER TWELVE

"iT's ALWAYs niCe to hAVe
SOMePLaCe To coME home to. At BeSt, it's
a pLAcE wHeRe yOU cAn ReSt aNd BE REfreSHeD
bY FAMiLiAR SuRROuNdinGs aNd weLL-loVeD PeOpLE.
AT wORSt, At LEASt yoU REmeMBeR wHy YOu
waNTed To gO aWAy ON ADVeNtUReS
iN THE FiRSt pLAce."

THE KING OF DRAGONFLIES'S palace was no longer
gloomy. Sleepy glowworms clung to the ceiling,
lighting every nook and cranny. The bodies of
the dragonflies blazed with color, and the beating of their
wings threw scatters of light everywhere.

In that brilliant group, squelching along in his wet
socks, Nurk might have felt very small and shabby, but
he was too tired and too proud, and it helped that every
dragonfly that caught his eye bowed very deeply to him.

"You *did* it!" Scatterwings hurtled out of the corner and
nearly bowled him over. She hugged Nurk. She hugged
Flicker. She hugged Nurk again. She grabbed one in each

set of arms and hugged them both simultaneously. Nurk gasped for air.

The King of Dragonflies came down from his throne and swept Flicker up in his arms. There was more hugging. Nurk glanced around and wondered if there was a corner he could crawl into and sleep for a week. Also, his socks were starting to bother him.

He was pretty sure that you weren't supposed to take your socks off in the middle of a throne room. But he realized that he didn't much care anymore. As the king was making a speech, Nurk sat down and peeled his socks off.

His hind paws were very soggy. Nurk wiggled his toes and wondered how long it would take for the Gorgeous Grape to wear off.

Silence fell. Nurk looked up. "What?"

Scatterwings started giggling and clamped a hand over her mouth.

"I said," said the king, "is there any way that we can repay you, young shrew? Anything at all?"

"I could really use a clean pair of socks," said Nurk. "And, sir—" He stood up, wringing his tail in his paws. "Sir, have you seen my grandmother? Scatterwings said you knew her . . ."

"Lady Surka? She was here some seasons ago. Three or four, I would say. But no, we have not seen her since." The king smiled. "She is always welcome in our lands, of course—her or any member of her family."

"Oh," said Nurk. Three or four seasons ago? He couldn't remember when the family had given her up for dead, but four seasons was a long time . . .

"Is there anything else, brave shrew?"

Nurk thought for a minute. "I think I'd like to go home now."

"Then we will have someone take you home," said the king, smiling. "And we will fetch you socks." He clapped his lower set of arms. A dragonfly hurried off and returned a few moments later with a velvet pillow.

Draped across the pillow was a pair of socks. They were golden at the toe, shading to orange at the heel, and a fiery red at the tops. They looked very warm. "Ooooh," Nurk said, impressed.

They were also about two sizes too big, but Nurk didn't care. He pulled them on happily.

"You are a friend of dragonflies, now and always," said the king, laying a hand on his shoulder. "You are always welcome in our kingdom, and if you should ever get stuck on a log again, any one of our people will be honored to help you."

"Thank you, sir," said Nurk.

"*Do* come back," said Scatterwings. "Please?"

"I will," Nurk promised. He hugged her and Prince Flicker and bowed to the king and Amberskeins. Then they bowed, and he bowed again, and the dragonfly warriors all saluted him, and there was a great deal of formality. Nurk was very glad to escape all the bowing and get back to his trusty Snailboat.

The nymphs towed him away from shore and upriver. The dragonflies had packed him a meal in a small picnic basket. The food was odd and crunchy and wrapped in paper-thin leaves, but it tasted good. Nurk ate a few bites, then curled up in the bottom of the Snailboat with his blanket and fell asleep.

He slept through the trip upriver and through the arrival of the giant carp, who hauled the Snailboat most of the way. He slept through the fields and the countryside, and he slept through the rapids, where the nymphs lifted the Snailboat out of the water and portaged it up the shore to the far side, and the carp flung itself up and over the rocks with a few thrusts of its powerful tail.

He woke up when one of the dragonfly nymphs reached into the Snailboat and shook his shoulder. "Hey," said the nymph, "wake up. You're home."

Nurk sat up, blinking. There was his own tree and

his own front door. The nymphs had tied the Snailboat neatly to one of the tree roots.

"Thank you," said Nurk. The nymph grinned at him and waved, then dived with a *plop!* into the stream.

Nurk watched as he swam out to two more nymphs.

"Your grandmother will be proud," said the big white carp.

Nurk turned, startled, and saw the enormous fish swimming in the shadow of the tree roots, tail undulating lazily against the current.

"*Will* be? But my grandmother—it's been so long—I think she's dead," said Nurk, surprised, and too tired to be tactful.

"Dead? *Surka*?" The carp gave a great bubbling laugh that threatened to swamp the boat. Nurk caught the rim of the shell as the Snailboat rocked. "She may die someday, same as the rest of us, but I wouldn't put money on it. She was very much alive two seasons ago, young shrew."

"She . . . what?" Nurk leaned over the edge of the Snailboat. "Only two seasons ago? But she's been gone for ages and ages . . . The dragonflies said . . . We all thought . . ."

The fin along the carp's back rippled in a shrug. "I don't know about that, but I wouldn't count her dead until I'd seen the body." He paused. "Actually, even then, I'd poke it a few times. Your grandmother's awfully tough, for a mammal."

Nurk's mind whirled. His grandmother, still alive? Really? Could the carp be right?

If so, then why hadn't she ever come back?

Where was she? Could he find her?

For a moment, Nurk wanted to leap to his feet, push the Snailboat away from the bank, and go find his grandmother right away.

Then he laughed to himself. He was so tired he could barely stand up, and he was hungry, and he had no clean socks left, except for the ones the dragonflies had given him.

"Can you tell me where you saw her last?" he asked the carp instead.

"Not far north of here. She was going upstream, along the bank at night, in the dark of the moon." The carp fanned his tail thoughtfully. "There's a stone there that looks like a pig. You can't miss it."

"Thank you," said Nurk.

"Anytime, young shrew," said the fish, and sunk below the water. Nurk watched a white shadow speed out into the middle of the stream, to the waiting nymphs.

All four waved, and the shrew waved back. Then they dived and swam away.

He opened his front door and went inside. In front of the portrait of Lady Surka, forever brandishing the severed head, he stopped.

"You'd be proud. You *will* be proud, Grandma,"

he said. "I had an adventure. Someday I'll tell you all about it."

One last time he opened the old diary. The leather was warm and smooth under his paws.

Near the end of the book, there was a drawing of a shrew and some strange shaggy creature, sitting together and sharing a meal.

i hAvE eNJoYed My StAy hERe. I hAVe MAde MaNY GOod FRieNdS aNd A FeW gooD eNEmieS, ANd i hOPE to ReTuRN SomeDaY.

FoR NoW, thoUGh, i Am BEginNinG To thiNK ABouT viSiTiNg HoMe. PaRTiaLLy, oF coURse, iS ThE neeD to GEt oUt oF towN bEFoRe thE ConStAbLEs FiNaLLy FiGuRe oUt wHeRe I aM, BUt ALso iT WOuLd BE gooD To sLEeP iN mY owN BEd aGAiN, eveN iF ThEy HAVE PROBAbLy tURnEd iT iNTo a gUeST BedROoM bY NoW.

Nurk smiled. He could see down the hall to the kitchen. On his kitchen table was a pile of the peculiar pastries that the salamanders made out of watercress and lily roots. His friends had left a gift to welcome him home.

The Snailboat bobbed quietly in the current, and the setting sun painted the stream all the colors of a really cool pair of socks. Nurk closed the door and went inside to have a pastry and a cheese sandwich.